Dr. Joseph MacInnis

FITZGERALD'S
STORM

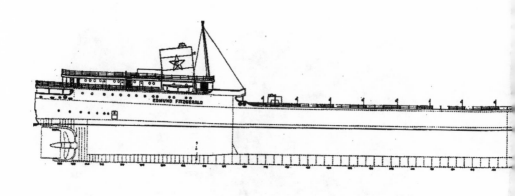

Dr. Joseph MacInnis

FITZGERALD'S
STORM

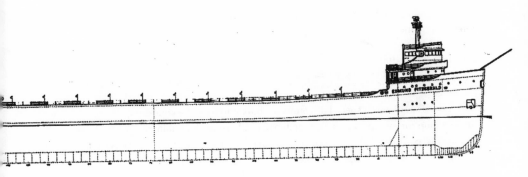

THE WRECK OF THE
EDMUND FITZGERALD

Macmillan Canada
Toronto

Canadian Cataloguing in Publication Data

MacInnis, Joseph, 1937–
  Fitzgerald's storm : the wreck of the Edmund Fitzgerald

ISBN 0-7715-7467-3

1. Edmund Fitzgerald (Ship) .   2. Shipwrecks – Superior,
Lake.   I. Title.

G530.E26M32 1997   977.4'9043   C97-931141-1

This book is available at special discounts for bulk purchases by your group or
organization for sales promotions, premiums, fundraising and seminars.
For details, contact: Macmillan Canada, Special Sales Department, 29 Birch Avenue,
Toronto, ON M4V 1E2. Tel: 416-963-8830.

Lyrics from "The Wreck of the Edmund Fitzgerald," which appear on pp. 7, 31, 38, 45,
52, 55, 60, 65, 76 and 77, reprinted with permission of Moose Music and Gordon
Lightfoot.

Front cover illustration and illustrations on pages 5, 89, and 132: David Conklin
Back cover photograph: Heidi Bassett-Blair
Cover and interior design: John Lee
Typesetting: Archetype

Macmillan Canada
A Division of Canada Publishing Corporation
Toronto, Ontario, Canada

1 2 3 4 5   TRI   01 00 99 98 97

Printed in Canada

Other books by Dr. Joseph MacInnis

Underwater Images
Underwater Man
The Land that Devours Ships
Titanic: In a New Light
Saving the Oceans

The Great Lakes iron ore tanker, the S.S. Edmund Fitzgerald, *was two city-blocks long.*

A lake...she is the earth's eye; looking into which the beholder measures the depth of his own nature.

—HENRY DAVID THOREAU

CONTENTS

SOUNDINGS

In 1991, I was the co-leader of an expedition to study and film the *Titanic*. Our 17 dives to her shattered remains in 12,500 feet of water allowed us to undertake a comprehensive scientific study and resulted in a CBS television special, an IMAX film, and a best-selling book.

After seeing the IMAX film *Titanica* and reading the book *Titanic: In a New Light*, the International Joint Commission — six commissioners appointed by the president of the United States and the prime minister of Canada to manage our shared lakes and rivers — asked me to develop a similar science education project focused on the five Great Lakes — Superior, Michigan, Huron, Erie, and Ontario — and the mighty Saint Lawrence River.

The Great Lakes are the most important natural resource shared by Canada and the United States. For more than two centuries these lakes and their outlet to the sea have been a food source, a water source, and a trading route for the two Canadian provinces and eight American states that surround them. Today, some 40 million people live within a day's drive of their 10,000 miles of shoreline. Like other freshwater ecosystems around the world, they are balanced between ailing health and imminent collapse, between the consequences of our mistakes and our commitment to restore their health.

The first science-educational element I proposed to the International Joint Commission was a series of "discovery dives." With the support of my friends at Harbor Branch Oceanographic Institution, we brought together a group of marine scientists, and Canadian and American high-school students in 1994 to explore some of the underwater highlights of this astonishing unsalted sea. Using Harbor Branch's ship, the *Edwin Link*, and a three-person research sub launched from her stern, we made dives at the intersection of the Saint Lawrence River and the Saguenay Fjord, the western end of Lake Ontario, off Long Point in Lake Erie, and in the eastern depths of Lake Superior.

Over a period of four weeks, we visited the shimmering home of beluga and minke whales, saw a disturbed lake bed that hinted of long-ago earthquakes, filmed an intact 19th-century schooner, and studied the fractured hull of a giant ore carrier in Lake Superior: the *Edmund Fitzgerald*.

Of all the dives, the most riveting were the ones we made to the *Edmund Fitzgerald*. Nineteen years earlier, the *Fitzgerald* had been overwhelmed by a hurricane-force storm and swallowed by the lake. She was as long as two city blocks, but she went under so quickly that none of her 29 crewmen had time to make a distress call. There were no survivors.

We spent three days studying the sundered ship lying under 530 feet of near-freezing water. She had been torn in half. Her bow section and stern section were separated by a huge area of lake floor filled with hundreds of pieces of ripped steel scattered between piles of cargo. There was no sun, only layers of darkness.

I was overwhelmed by questions. Why did a 13,000-ton ship carrying 26,000 tons of cargo and 29 men sink so quickly? What was it like for the officers and the crew as their great ship, this symbol of stability, came apart under the forces of nature? What became of the wives and children the men left behind? How would I behave if confronted by those same lethal forces?

In many ways the *Fitzgerald* story is our relationship to the Great Lakes writ large. It contains elements of heroism and humility as well as ignorance and arrogance. It features people who look at life with wonder and others who are so busy stripping things apart that life's fascinating complexities are reduced to trifles not worth bothering about.

Shipwrecks are like dreams, lying beyond the observable everyday world. Like the dark waters they lie in, they are reminders of our long engagement with the natural world. They draw us into places we do not belong, confirming that there are times when reason and fact are no match for enduring mysteries.

⚓

In mid-November, four months after we made our dives to the wreck site, I sailed across Lake Superior and down the length of Lake Huron on the *Seaway Queen*, a proud old freighter the same age and general dimensions as the *Fitzgerald*. Her captain and crew took me through every part of their ship. We ran into severe winds and high seas on both lakes. Coupled with my own 30 years of seafaring on working ships, the voyage helped me to better understand the behavior of freshwater freighters and the good people who guide them.

In July 1995, a year after my first look at the wreckage, I went out to the *Fitzgerald* site to make my second dive to the drowned ship. Four of us were in an all-weather boat moving at 30 knots across the water. Distance blurred the shoreline so that the lake looked like the floor of the sky. The late-evening sun was hidden behind clouds fringed with gold. It was almost dark.

We had just come out of Whitefish Bay into the main body of Lake Superior. The black waves ahead of us were ridged like sharks' teeth. On the northern horizon we could see the outlines of a Canadian navy ship and next to it a large tugboat. In the depths below lay the shattered steel bones of the *Fitzgerald*.

As we approached the two ships, their anchor lights changed from the size of distant stars to radiant spheres high on their mastheads. On the stern of the navy ship, *HMCS Cormorant*, was a small submarine whose steel-pressure hull and thick viewports made a powerful statement about the physics of deep water. Down there the laws of the land do not apply.

We slowed almost to a stop and prepared to board the *Cormorant*. The water was smooth and black, reflecting a river of stars. For a moment I felt weightless. The water and the sky below me were an enormous presence, older and harder to decipher than human consciousness. As I looked into it, I thought I could see the outline of a big freighter heading west.

PART ONE

THE GALES OF NOVEMBER

The legend lives on from the Chippewa on down
of the big lake they called Gitche Gumee...

It is a lake born of fire, its origins reaching back into deep time about a thousand million years ago when the center of what was to become North America was being pulled apart, and massive plumes of basaltic lava with an internal temperature of some two thousand degrees Fahrenheit rose up from the interior.

The thousands of basaltic, rhyolite, and gabbroic flows moved stunning quantities of material from beneath the yet-to-be-formed lake bed. Eventually, the earth's crust sagged into a wide depression. Then, millions of years of sediments, mostly eroded from mountains to the east, were deposited in this ever-deepening depression. Much later, the first of the great ice sheets descended from the north and began biting into the sediments.

The events that gave Lake Superior its present deepwater shape began about two million years ago when the first of at least four gigantic glaciers shuddered out of the Arctic and pressed down on the northern half of North America. The last of these, the Wisconsin, began its southward advance about 115,000 years ago. One of its slowly expanding fronts, which geologists later called the Superior Lobe, crept out of the northeast and aimed itself at the midsection of the continent.

The advancing ice was higher than the Grand Canyon. Its weight and the granite teeth it had torn off the hills at higher latitudes changed the face of the earth beneath it, scouring, stripping, grinding, pulverizing even the hardest rocks that lay in its path. At what is now the shoreline of the world's widest lake, the glacier found a weakness in the earth's crust and descended. Where there is now water there was once ice hundreds of fathoms deep, gouging out thousands of square miles of soft sandstone, siltstone, and shale. When the earth warmed and the ice retreated, left behind was a lake configured in the shape of a gigantic wolf's head: the wolf's mouth is the Keweenaw Peninsula; Isle Royale is its slanted eye; where the great lake narrows toward Duluth is the animal's long, pointed nose. Within the lake's oceanic vastness lies one-tenth of the world's liquid fresh water.

⊥

Early French explorers called it *le Lac Supérieure*, the upper lake. They
sensed its great size and unpredictability and kept their voyageur canoes
close to shore. If they had paddled 20 miles a day, it would have taken
them three months to see its 1,700 miles of heavily forested shoreline.

In the 1800s, the first of thousands of lumbermen surrounded the
great waters and began to clear-cut the ocean of trees that covered
Minnesota, Wisconsin, and Michigan, turning pine and spruce and
cedar into ships and houses for an expanding nation. In the 1840s, the
financial allure of copper drew miners from England and Germany to
dig hundreds of miles of tunnels into the bedrock of the Keweenaw
Peninsula. They were followed by men who tunneled and blasted and
hauled the ore that could be turned into iron. Shore towns like Duluth,
Marquette, and Sault Ste. Marie appeared. Lake Superior became a
blue-water highway.

Sailing on the big lake, especially in wooden schooners, was a high-
risk enterprise. The lake was almost 400 miles from east to west and
at one point was 160 miles from north to south. There were few safe
harbors. Winters were long and intense and summers were short. Even
in August the water was cold enough to paralyze anyone who fell overboard. In the fall, fast-moving storms spawned oceanlike gales with
20-foot waves. Many captains called it the world's most dangerous body
of water.

According to historian Julius Wolff, Superior's first recorded shipwreck was the schooner *Invincible*, which foundered in a storm off
Whitefish Point in 1816. Since then, more than 350 ships have come to
rest in its shallows and in its depths.

For the Ojibway, the first people on its eastern shore, Gitche Gumee
was more than a horizon-spanning lake fed by 200 rivers. It had a
gleaming liquid face. It had a body that seemed to breathe and was
always in motion. It had hundreds of moods, each with a different name.
For the first people, the mother of all lakes was alive.

Chapter One

LOADING THE
LAST CARGO

Lake Superior, Sunday, November 9, 1975
Just before dawn, a faint gleam rose out of the east, lighting the world from below. The light slowly increased, bleaching the sky, revealing a thin line of clouds. The surface of the lake was calm and gunflint gray.

A long, low shape formed on the lake's eastern horizon. It grew, its tiny dots of lights taking on solidity: red to port, green to starboard, and two white pinpricks on its bow and stern mastheads. The lights moved steadily closer and suddenly the shape loomed over the water and the lake parted, sliced by a wedge of red steel. On each side, waves appeared, curling, white, and thunderous. For long seconds a high steel cliff stormed by, pressing back the weight of the lake. As soon as the last of the steel moved on, the lake closed in, furious and writhing. Slowly the lake subsided into its original skin of heaving black.

There were 29 lake sailors on board the *Edmund Fitzgerald* that morning. They were a cross section of Middle America, young and old and middle-aged men with addresses in Minnesota, Ohio, Florida, Pennsylvania, and Wisconsin. Some of the men were the sons of former sailors. Some were spending their first season working on the lakes. The crewmen were divided into those who lived forward and those who lived aft.

The men who lived in the forward part of the ship—Jack McCarthy, James Pratt, Michael Armagost, Gene O'Brien, John Poviach, and the others—were officers, wheelsmen, and deckhands. Those with quarters in the stern—George Holl, Ed Bindson, Buck Champeau, Tom Bentsen, Russ Haskell, and their friends—were stewards, engineers, and oilers.

The Edmund Fitzgerald, *on a calm day.*   Photo: Bob Campbell

For all of them, the *Fitzgerald* was both office and home. For a few of them, it was the only real home they had.

The *Fitzgerald* was as big as a 72-story skyscraper, lying on its side. Like a skyscraper she had four outer walls that formed her hull. She was long and narrow. She had corridors called passageways and inner walls called partitions and bulkheads. But unlike a building, the *Fitzgerald* moved at a speed of 18 knots.

A sailor new to the *Fitzgerald* had to learn his way around this complicated all-steel world. The uppermost deck that runs the entire length of the ship from bow to stern is known as the main deck, the weather or the spar deck. The intersection of the main deck with the side of the hull is called the gunwale. The intersection of the side plating with the bottom plating is the bilge. Some compartments are called rooms, such as stateroom and engine room, but generally speaking, the word *room* isn't used. The place where the ordinary sailor eats is the mess deck.

The second thing a new sailor learned was that every task aboard a big ship like the *Fitzgerald* posed some danger. Going to sea involved working with powerful machinery, high-pressure steam, volatile fuels, heavy lifts, stepped-up electrical voltages, and unpredictable weather. The novice crewman would quickly learn that on a big diesel ship you are exposed and vulnerable. Sometimes you breathe heavy fumes. Sometimes you fight diesel fires. Inside the engine room, either you wear protective ear covers or, in six months, you'll be as deaf as a stone. It's easy to burn your arms or legs; one slip and your shin is hard against a hot exhaust line or your shoulder is tight against a steam line and your skin is sizzling like bacon fat.

Men fall on big ships. They trip on steel combings and tear up an ankle. They tumble down a stairwell and tear open a knee. In the darkness of a deep storm, a hatch cover comes ajar and they walk over an open edge and are killed by the long fall into the iron hold.

The older members of the *Fitzgerald*'s crew had seen every kind of accident: the new sailor who fractured his skull because he failed to duck going through a steel doorway; the nylon mooring line that tightened on a man's leg and imploded his tibia; the winch that crushed a deckhand's forearm, leaving his muscles crimson and hanging.

The new sailor learned that the most sacred thing in a ship is her watertight integrity. He discovered which compartments are watertight and which are not. He memorized the location of all watertight doors and all watertight hatches. Within a short time of his arrival, he knew that wherever water, steam, electrical cables, or ventilation ducts go through a watertight bulkhead or deck, the hole is plugged by a stuffing tube or other device to prevent leakage.

Sailors were drawn to the seafaring life for the flowing beauties of the big lakes, for the love-hate relationship with their big ship and the friends they lived and worked with. Central to their existence was the man they called captain. Captain Ernest R. McSorley, 62, was born in Ogdensburg, New York, a small town that overlooks the south shore of the Saint Lawrence River. As a boy he had gazed out at the parade of ships passing and dreamed of a future command. At age 18, he signed on his first ship as a deckhand. At age 25, he joined the Columbia Transportation Company as a wheelsman. In the years that followed, McSorley worked his way up to third, second, and then first mate. In 1951, at age 37, he became the youngest master on the lakes. After 34 years with Columbia, he was given command of the "Big Fitz." The year was 1972.

McSorley was of medium height, round-shouldered and muscular. His face was thin and angular and his jet-black hair was combed straight back from a receding widow's peak. An aquiline nose jutted out over a firm mouth. When he spoke to his men, his dark eyes looked directly at them as if in a dare. McSorley had been married for a long time but had no children. His men described him as quiet, intense, and very competent. He had big hands that had coiled hundreds of miles of lines, turned the wheels of dozens of ships, written 40 years' worth of ships' logs, and felt the sting of winter gales.

Like every man who rises through the ranks to take command of a Great Lakes freighter, Ernest McSorley knew the meaning of leadership. To be a good leader on a ship as big as the *Fitzgerald*, he had to have willing followers. He had to inspire his men, not order them. Commanding a man to do a difficult task was a last resort.

In the 1970s, the men who sailed the Great Lakes were better educated than their predecessors. Almost all of them had gone to high school. Some had a year or more of college. A few of them were smarter than the men who outranked them. Educated men needed to know how things worked, and why, so McSorley took the time to reveal his knowledge of the ship to them.

McSorley knew the strengths and weaknesses of his officers and men. He praised them in public and reprimanded them in private. He respected their problems and offered them guidance. But he took great pains not to fall into the trap of becoming one of the gang. He kept his distance, aware that if a breach of discipline arose, or if they found themselves in a life-threatening situation, his men had to respect his position.

Early in the morning of November 9, 1975, McSorley's ship was empty and riding high. For the trip across the lake, the ballast tanks of the *Fitzgerald* had been filled with water to give her the desired draft and trim for this time of year. She was making 18 knots on a western heading of 248 degrees that would take her to the entrance of the Duluth-Superior Harbor.

The trio of men standing watch in her pilothouse were not fooled by the past few days of unseasonably warm weather and the uncommonly clear sky. They knew that the mood of the world's widest lake could darken quickly, especially in November. They knew that Superior was so big it created its own weather.

At 7:00 a.m., the *Fitzgerald* was moored alongside the Burlington Northern Railroad Dock in Superior, Wisconsin. The officer standing in her pilothouse looked out across an immense enclosed harbor whose waters were calm and channeled with a pale Indian-summer light. To the north lay the Minnesota shore and the misty blue outline of the city of Duluth. Built where the Saint Louis River and the riches of mine and prairie flowed in from the West, the harbor with its long parade of docks, silos, and warehouses shipped some 40 million tons of cargo each year, mostly coal, grain, and iron ore.

The American steel industry emerged from World War II as the largest, most modern steel industry on earth, a position it maintained for more than two decades. It was a sprawling world of open-pit mines, blast furnaces, rolling mills, and casting machines that burned huge amounts of energy, and was dependent on the mass labor of thousands of steelworkers. In 1975, Americans were consuming the equivalent of four Great Pyramids of solid steel a year. Critical to its production was a steady flow of iron ore being shipped from the mines to the furnaces in the south.

The *Fitzgerald* was moored with its starboard flank in the shadow of a row of concrete storage bins built into the dock. Most of the bins held 300 tons. Some held smaller amounts. Each had its own loading chute, which was lowered into the ship's open hatches.

A view of the Edmund Fitzgerald's *main deck.*   Photo: Ruth Hudson

Running the full length of the *Fitzgerald*'s main deck were 21 rectangular hatch openings. A single piece of sheet steel, as thick as a man's finger and the size of a driveway, was laid down on a rim of steel around each hatch opening and secured with 68 manually closed Kestner clamps. Every hatch cover weighed seven tons and required the use of a mobile deck crane or "iron deck hand" to remove it.

Loading and simultaneously deballasting tons of water from the *Fitzgerald* was the responsibility of the chief mate, Jack McCarthy. About the same height but slimmer than his old friend Ernest McSorley, McCarthy looked out on the world through a pair of steel-rimmed glasses. Everyone liked him. He had grown up in Pittsburgh, Pennsylvania, inheriting from his devout Irish Catholic parents a sly sense of humor and a deft way with words. At one point in his life, he'd seriously considered becoming a writer.

McCarthy was 22 years old in 1935, when he signed on his first Great Lakes ship, the bulk carrier *Yosemite*. Seven years later he married the sister of a shipmate and joined the Columbia Transportation Division of Oglebay Norton. In the years that followed he had four children and worked his way up through the ranks of the Columbia fleet. It was while he was working on the *Sensibar* that he first met McSorley, beginning a friendship that would endure for decades.

Eventually, McCarthy was given his first command, the *Joseph H. Frantz*, which at one time had been the company's flagship. Then, in the summer of 1956, Jack McCarthy sailed out of Marblehead Harbor on the southwestern shore of Lake Erie and missed his turn. He was supposed to head east into the open lake, but steered north long enough for the keel of his freighter, the *Ben E. Tate*, to find the rocks of Kelley's Island and tear a huge hole in her bottom. There was a shudder, the sounds of wounded metal and astonished men. It cost almost a quarter of a million dollars to tow the *Tate* back to shore and repair her innards and hull plates.

First Mate Jack McCarthy in the Fitzgerald's *pilothouse.*

Photo: John McCarthy

McCarthy was devastated. A few months after the Coast Guard hearing, he was back at work — but not as a captain. Later, after a period of redemption, he became the captain of the *Sylvania* and then the *Tomlinson* of the Columbia fleet. On this voyage, he had signed on as first mate so he could work with his long-time shipmate, Ernest McSorley.

At 7:30 a.m., on November 9, 1975, Jack McCarthy and the men working for him were preparing to load the first iron ore into the hatch closest to the stern. Farther up the deck a four-man team rolled the hatch crane forward to the next hatch. Moving on parallel tracks, the crane straddled the width of the deck like a gigantic table. After the crane was positioned, the men attached four steel lift cables to the corner of each hatch cover. Then they slowly raised the seven-ton cover and placed it in the space between the hatches. On McCarthy's signal, the loader on the dock released the clutch and lowered the chute, braking to slow its descent so that it came to rest gently on the edge of the hatch. He did this carefully; if the chute landed too hard, it could affect the watertight integrity of the hatch cover. A few seconds later, another dock worker reached over to open the door of the chute and the first of millions of taconite pellets stormed into the hold.

Taconite is a low-grade iron ore that is crushed, ground, and concentrated into round balls the size of marbles then kiln-fired to 2,400 degrees Fahrenheit. The reddish-brown pellets are easily handled in chutes, conveyor belts, railway cars, and cargo holds. Packed together, they are twice as dense as water. At first, the pellets roaring into hatch 21 fell the height of a three-story building and bounced like hailstones off the steel floor. Dust began to rise and the pellets quickly formed into a small hill growing inside its own thunder.

The enlarging hill of iron ore and the 20 others that would be built up in the next five hours were bound for Detroit and an immense steel mill that ran for three miles along the waterfront. In a process that involved the fiercest and largest manufacturing engines on the planet, the taconite would be joined with coke in blast furnaces, emerge as liquid iron, go into another furnace, and be transformed into liquid carbon steel and then into red hot ingots and slabs, and finally through high-pressure hot and cold rolling machines into sheet steel. The process was choreographed in huge black rooms that stank of slag and carbon smoke and were filled with men in spark-proof jackets, steel-toed boots, and dark glasses clipped to their hard hats. Steel men respect hot steel like a mariner respects dark water.

One after the other, each hatch on the *Fitzgerald* was filled with 300 tons of pellets. When all 21 hatches were loaded with this amount, the ship was slipped backward to line up the next row of chutes. Starting again at the stern, another 300 tons was poured down into each hatch. During the loading it was critical that the ship be kept level in the water. As the tons of pellets roared in and slammed against the bottom plates, McCarthy kept looking up at the red, green, and white trim lights mounted high on the *Fitzgerald*'s stern deckhouse. A green light indicated a list to starboard, a red light to port. A white light meant that the ship was level. At the end of the second filling of all the hatches, some 1,500 tons of ore were added to the after hold. This would put more weight in the stern and give the ship's propeller more bite. When the last of the pellets rolled down the chute, McCarthy decided to stop loading while he emptied the ship's ballast tanks, the huge water-filled spaces that ran along the bottom and submerged sides of the ship.

In the forward part of her engine room, the *Fitzgerald* had four electrically driven ballast pumps. Working together, they could pump 7,500 gallons a minute. The ship also had two auxiliary pumps that could move 4,000 gallons a minute. McCarthy's usual practice was to use the two auxiliaries to de-ballast the *Fitzgerald*. After the last of the ballast water was pumped overboard and the ship was riding higher, he and his deckhands continued the loading of taconite until the holds were full.

The *Fitzgerald* was completely loaded a few minutes after 1:00 p.m. Her holds now contained some 26,116 tons of iron ore. The white-painted numbers on her bow and stern confirmed that her keel was now at a depth of slightly more than 27 feet. When the *Fitzgerald* was commissioned in 1958, the Coast Guard had strict regulations to prevent ships of her size from being overloaded: there had to be a specific height or freeboard between the surface of the water and the level of the *Fitzgerald*'s main deck. It was believed that this freeboard would keep the ship's deck above the biggest waves generated in a severe storm.

Initially, the minimum required freeboard at her midships was 12 feet, ½ inches in summer, and 14 feet, 3½ inches in winter. After considerable lobbying by the Lake Carriers Association, the requirements were eventually reduced three times. In 1973, the *Fitzgerald*'s minimum required freeboard became 11 feet, 2 inches in summer, and 11 feet, 6 inches in winter. After 17 seasons of hard toil, the *Fitzgerald* could now be legally loaded with more ore in winter than she could during her first summer.

As McCarthy signed off and handed over the final freeboard readings to the loading dock manager, his deck crew laid down the last hatch cover and secured it. Once in place the cover was bolted down tightly. It took two men with a clamp wrench about 30 minutes to secure each hatch.

Among the deckhands tightening the clamps that Sunday morning was one of the youngest members of the crew, 22-year-old Bruce Lee Hudson. Hudson had long black hair, mischievous eyes, and an athletic body. In 1974, after a year as a construction worker in Atlanta, he was hired on to work in the engine room of the bulk freighter *Ashland*. That winter, while his ship was berthed in Toledo, he stayed on board as the ship keeper. In April 1975, he signed on as a deckhand on Columbia's flagship, the *Edmund Fitzgerald*.

Hudson loved his newfound profession. When you worked as a lake sailor you made close friends. Your room and board were free and there was a chance to save money. A good son, Hudson shared part of his salary with his parents, Ruth and Oddis. He spent some of it on a new stereo system for his small room in the after part of the ship. But his best investment, the one that gave him an adrenaline rush, was his gleaming, all-electric-blue, road-hugging Kawasaki motorcycle.

Bruce Hudson (left) and Karl Peckol on the Fitzgerald's *main deck.*

Photo: Ruth Hudson

For Hudson, the big, straight-deck ship that he lived and worked on was still a mystery. Guiding it through a fog, passing other ships, plotting a course, firing a boiler, reading the radar, and interpreting weather forecasts were complex acts brooded over by older men. There were so many soul-stirring experiences: solitary, sensuous moments on deck in the warm summer rain; cold autumn nights under the purity and peace of the northern lights. In spite of its often weary routine, life on a big ship held a spark of glamour impossible to find in a bank or a service station.

Besides Hudson, there were several other men on the *Fitzgerald* who were in their twenties, including Karl Peckol and Hudson's roommate, Dave Weiss, a cadet from the Great Lakes Maritime Academy. They were all good friends. When they worked as deckhands, they kept the ship clean by sweeping, painting, chipping and coiling, and stowing lines. When they worked as watchmen or wheelsmen, they monitored machinery or took their turn in the pilothouse, steering the ship under an officer's command. One of the benefits of being a sailor was that it taught you self-discipline and responsibility. Another was that it forced you to make a pact of fidelity with the ship and with your mates.

The *Fitzgerald*'s operating routine was built around its three major activities: traveling across the lakes, transiting canals and locks, and tying up in ports to transfer cargo. Each morning the daily schedule was prepared by the first mate and posted on bulletin boards throughout the ship. It named the duty officers assigned to various watches and included changes to the ship's normal routine such as lifeboat drills, fire drills, walk-through inspections, training schedules, and work-party assignments.

Sailors new to the *Fitzgerald* soon learned that getting along meant more than learning new duties, obeying the rules, and standing watches. It meant living and working with a group of people who were confined to a ship and crowded into small spaces. It meant long hours and some-times extreme working conditions of intense heat and bitter cold. Regardless of age or experience, going to sea meant showing respect and tolerance for everyone else on board. There were moments when this respect moved into uncharted latitudes: when someone was hurt or trapped or in trouble and someone else stepped forward and put his life on the line to help out. At those times, they were a brotherhood. It was the most glorious thing about life at sea.

The men in their twenties listened with deference when the chairs in the mess room were pulled in closer and the older men lit their cigarettes and began to tell stories. There was the one about the captain who drank or the mate who was killed in a fall. There was the great storm of 1913 and the close call on northern Lake Michigan. There was the November 1966 blizzard that broke the 660-foot *Daniel J. Morrell* into two pieces that floated briefly then vanished into the icy waters of Lake Huron. The room filled with smoke. The yarns continued. But to Hudson and his friends, these were other ships sailed by other men in other times.

It was almost 2:00 p.m. on that November Sunday when the *Fitzgerald* cruised through the pole-mounted red and green lights marking the passage through the Superior breakwall. She was riding low in the water, steaming at six knots, the red steel cliff of her hull more formidable for being unbroken by portholes.

After the *Fitzgerald* passed through the breakwall, she began to pick up speed. A thin black ribbon of smoke unrolled from her funnel. The blue-gray lake lay still. A white ribbon of foam, as straight as the ship's keel, hissed out from below the stern, agitated the surface of the lake, and then vanished like a phantom.

Chapter Two

I CHRISTEN YOU
EDMUND
FITZGERALD

In 1957, there was talk of the Russians launching the world's first space satellite, and President Eisenhower sending in troops to control the racial violence in Little Rock, Arkansas. In Detroit, the Ford Motor Company was launching its brand-new Edsel and a labor leader by the name of Jimmy Hoffa was bullying his way to the top of the International Brotherhood of Teamsters.

When the building of the largest and longest bulk carrier on the Great Lakes was announced, the news attracted national attention. The *Edmund Fitzgerald* was to be 729 feet long, within a foot of the maximum length allowed for passage through the soon-to-be-completed Saint Lawrence Seaway. The ship would be 75 feet wide and have a capacity of 26,000 gross tons at a 27-foot draft. She would be coal-driven and her top speed would be 16 miles an hour, faster than most of the existing lake fleet.

The new ship would be the first vessel built by an American life insurance company as an investment. It would cost eight million dollars. Northwestern Mutual Life president and CEO Edmund Fitzgerald pointed out that some two-thirds of the 337 bulk carriers in the U.S. flag fleet on the lakes were more than 40 years old. "Not only is the new ship a sound financial investment," he said, "but it is an opportunity for our company to make a definite contribution to the national economy."

Like all cargo ships, the *Fitzgerald* was designed with one purpose: to carry her cargo efficiently and remain stable and buoyant. This mantra of efficiency and safety that started in the minds of the owner was passed on to the naval architect. After months of revisions, hundreds of hand-drawn blueprints were created to guide the day-to-day construction of the ship.

On August 9, 1957, a giant crane in Detroit's Rouge River shipyard swung the first keel plate into place. The most unusual feature of Hull 301, as it was then called, was the way it would be built. In the past, the procedure was to lay down the keel and the adjoining bottom plates then build up the sides and interior piece by piece. The process was expensive and time-consuming and forced welders and workers to toil in cramped, airless corners often with their tools over their heads. Cost-conscious shipwrights decided to borrow an assembly-line technique from the auto industry. Large sections of the hull, some weighing as much as 70 tons, would be built upside down in other parts of the yard then lifted into place by two huge mobile cranes.

Construction started with sheet and bar steel, trainloads of it, arriving at the head of the yard where it was stacked in the stockyard to await cleaning and delivery to the plate shop. The first bottom shell plates were laid down in the center of one of the building berths and welded together by an automatic welding machine. The new ship grew outward from her midships, where she was widest, towards her bow and stern. Her bilge and her ballast tanks were formed when a second layer of steel plates were laid on top of the

Stern view of the Fitzgerald.
Photo: Dossin Great Lakes Museum

first. The frames that separated the two layers were as high as a man is tall, with oval openings that allowed the bilge water and ballast water to run between them.

A short distance from the ship, under the high overhead lights of the steel hall, the big plates were cut, shaped, and welded into flat panels or stiffeners. These sub-assemblies were rolled outside the hall to be welded into larger three-dimensional sections. When completed, these sections, including stern decks, side tanks, bunker tanks, the forefoot, and the after-peak, were lifted across the yard by the gantry cranes and integrated into the emerging form that was becoming an ore carrier.

In April 1958, the board of trustees of Northwestern Mutual Life announced that Edmund Fitzgerald, president since 1947, was stepping down as the company's chief executive officer and that the new ship would be named in his honor.

Fitzgerald was a name long associated with ships and shipping on the Great Lakes. Edmund Fitzgerald's grandfather, John Fitzgerald, and his five brothers had been captains of Great Lakes sailing ships. His grandfather and his father were successive presidents of the Milwaukee Drydock Company. In spite of this maritime heritage, Edmund Fitzgerald was uneasy about the honor. "It is almost embarrassing," he told a reporter "to have such a magnificent vessel as a namesake."

Nine months after they laid down the first section of her keel, the gangs of men working in the yard, wearing thick windbreakers and wool hats for protection against the river's winds, looked up at the gray sky and saw the full outline of their ship. Most of her hull plates had been riveted and welded. She had an almost vertical bow and an upcurving cruiser stern. Her wide main deck, shaft tunnel, watertight bulkheads, and ballast manifolds were in position. Her rudder looked like the side of a barn and weighed 23 tons. Her bronze propeller was almost 20 feet in diameter and weighed 16 tons. In the weeks that followed, her 140-ton main engine and two 84-ton steam-fired boilers were lowered into her stern. Huge sections of her fore and aft cabins were hoisted more than 50 feet to the decks and welded into place.

Elizabeth and Edmund Fitzgerald on the main deck.

Photo: courtesy Captain Fred Leete

The launching of the largest man-made object ever dropped into fresh water took place on June 7, 1958, in front of a crowd of 15,000 spectators. It was a warm Saturday. They came by the hundreds in shirt-sleeves and light cotton dresses to fill two specially constructed grand-stands. Some sat on the roofs of nearby buildings. Some lined the piers. Large groups of the 900 men who built the new ship climbed onto the huge cranes or stood on piles of steel and lumber. Hundreds of others watched from the largest collection of watercraft — yachts, sailboats, scows, fishing boats, and tugs — ever assembled on the Detroit River.

An elevated wooden platform stood next to the bow of the ship. Red, white, and blue banners fluttered from its railings. It was filled with sev-eral rows of white-shirted bankers and politicians. After the prayers and the speeches, Elizabeth Fitzgerald, wife to Edmund, stepped up to the microphone. She was wearing a dark blue dress, white gloves, and a white pillbox hat with a thin net that covered her forehead. She looked out at the hushed crowd, over at her husband, and up at the cliff of red steel. Then she spoke: "I christen you *Edmund Fitzgerald*...God bless you."

She paused briefly and then swung the ribboned bottle of champagne with her left hand. It broke against the stem of the bow. White foam burst against the steel and ran down the side of the ship.

In the shadows below the platform holding the trustees and presi-dents and bankers, a line of gaunt men in soiled shirts watched as eight electronically controlled steel guillotines rammed down and cut the five-inch ropes holding the ship. There was a shout and a deep rumbling noise and the massive thing above them began to slide sideways toward the water.

Driven by gravity, the *Fitzgerald*'s first journey was down some 60 feet of slanting wood timbers smeared with train oil. Slowly she accelerated, snapping off the ends of huge logs. She hit the water with a scream of friction that turned into thunder. Her sideways entry sent a huge wave racing across the narrow basin. White and breaking, it climbed the retaining wall, splashing the crowd. Her flat bottom dug in deeply. Her top half began to roll. She rolled so far that some people in the crowd believed she might not recover. Slowly she came back up and rolled in the opposite direction. After another roll and then another she steadied, putting a heavy strain on the tug and the thick manila ropes that held her.

Even before the *Fitzgerald* hit the water, a sound rose from the shore-line. Thousands of voices were shouting and cheering in unison. On the roofs, along the piers, and in the grandstands, men and women were on

Side view of the Fitzgerald *during the launch.*

their feet, waving their hats and their flags. As the sound grew, it was overtaken by a new sound, a chorus of factory whistles, deep-throated boat horns, and two helicopters hovering overhead.

The next day the *Detroit News* ran a headline: BIGGEST SHIP ON THE LAKES IS LAUNCHED...It was followed by a three-column article and a picture of Mrs. Elizabeth Fitzgerald in her dark silk suit and white pillbox hat. Hidden in a corner of one of the back pages was another smaller article with the headline: SPECTATOR DIES AS SHIP IS LAUNCHED..."Stricken with a heart attack...Jennings Frazier, 58, of Toledo died at the scene...He attended the ceremonies with his wife, Ann Belle...They had come to Detroit at the invitation of their son, Stephen, an engineer on the freighter *Armco*."

Shortly after the launching, the *Fitzgerald* was towed to her fitting-out berth, a nearby concrete seawall under one of the giant shipyard cranes. During the summer, swarms of yardmen climbed on board to install the potable water system, fire sprinklers, the air-conditioning and refrigeration plants, and the galley, dining rooms, and crew quarters. Fifty-person lifeboats with their launching davits were cradled on the port and starboard side of the poop deck. Miles of electrical wire and cable were laid, most of it inside the bulkheads that surrounded the engine room, but much of it leading forward to the elevated pilot-house and a bank of electrical panels in the navigation bridge and chart room.

The *Fitzgerald* was made of steel to carry steel, but she also had to house and feed a working crew of 35 men, including eight officers. The white-painted deckhouse on her stern was built over her engine room and surrounded her big, raked smokestack. Its lower deck held a laundry room; a recreation room with a library, writing desk, and television set; the crew's mess with its long bolted tables and benches; a dark wood-paneled officers' dining room; and a spacious steel galley. The galley, which ran almost half the width of the ship, featured a wide-bodied gas stove flanked by electric freezers, dishwashers, and gleaming serving surfaces. The deck above held an office and living quarters for the chief engineer and accommodation for the three assistant engineers and the ordinary seamen. Each licensed officer had his own bedroom with a bathroom. The rest of the men lived two to a room with a shared bathroom.

The forward deckhouse rose like a white-painted castle over the bow of the ship. Its three decks—spar, foc'sle, and Texas—were lined with portholes and windows. On the lowest, or spar deck, was a recreation room, laundry room, and quarters for the ordinary seamen. Above it, on the foc'sle deck, were two well-appointed guest cabins featuring twin beds, tiled bathrooms, and deep pile carpet. A roomy guest lounge ran between them, its large wall window giving a panoramic view of the 21 cargo hatches and, in the distance, the white deckhouse towering over the stern.

The captain or master had his office and living quarters on this deck. As befits the managing director of an eight-million-dollar asset, his accommodations were both lavish and comfortable. The furniture, including the wide walnut desk and its sea-blue leather swivel chair, was bolted to the floor. Every mahogany drawer had a flip-lock to prevent the ship's motion from throwing it open.

The highest workspace on the ship was the pilothouse on the Texas deck. It was ringed with 31 large, wooden-frame windows that gave a spectacular view of water and sky. Its aftersection held a chart room filled with chart table, bookshelves, and drawers of nautical charts. Its foresection contained an array of radars, compasses, wind-speed indicators, telephones, a control console, and a docking telegraph. Behind the big wood-spoked wheel was the wheelsman's platform with metal railing all round to give protection in heavy seas.

Before the *Fitzgerald* could put to sea, hundreds of items had to be inspected and tested by the shipyard engineers. Her boilers were fired with coal and her main engine, a 7,500-horsepower steam turbine, was run in. As her mooring lines tightened, the ship's four-blade bronze propeller was slowly turned over. A gang of clipboard-carrying surveyors from the American Bureau of Shipping came on board to inspect her navigation lights, foghorn, and fire-fighting and lifesaving equipment and to ensure that the statutory load line was marked on her side amidships.

Every ship had its Plimsoll line, a column of horizontal marks on both sides indicating the levels that may be loaded for varying sea conditions. The line is named for Samuel Plimsoll, a short-tempered British parliamentarian and passionate champion of safety at sea. Plimsoll's target was the 19th-century shipowners who sent their overloaded, unseaworthy vessels into the Atlantic, hoping for a storm and a hefty insurance claim. In those days, overloading was a common practice and many good ships and many good men were lost because of it.

When the last worker closed the lid of his toolbox and walked down the accommodation ladder, he left behind a straight-decked leviathan

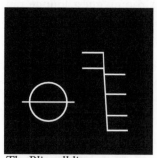

The Plimsoll line.

that weighed 13,000 gross tons and was two city blocks long and as wide as a three-lane highway. Most of the *Fitzgerald*'s length was occupied by the space for cargo, a spectacularly long, high-ceiling warehouse that was wide enough to accommodate four side by side railway trains and long enough to hold two football fields. The space was divided into three enormous sections by floor-to-ceiling, non-watertight screen bulkheads. When the three cargo holds were filled to capacity, they would contain enough raw iron to manufacture 7,500 automobiles.

When the *Fitzgerald* was completed and tested, she was ready to sail into a blue-water world that dominated the eastern half of North America. The five Great Lakes — Superior, Michigan, Huron, Erie,

Ontario—cover 95,000 square miles, making them the greatest expanse of fresh water on the planet. Ontario, the smallest, still ranks a respectable fourteenth among the world's largest lakes. Erie, Michigan, and Huron rank twelfth, sixth, and fifth, respectively. By any definition, Superior, big enough to contain the other four, is a freshwater ocean unto itself.

With their enormous expanse and vast heat capacity, the great waters play an important role as weather makers. In spring, they cool and calm the ocean of air flowing over them, dampening the tornado-spawning storms roaring in from the Midwest. In fall and early winter, their role reverses. The colossal heat they store up during the summer is released into the cold atmosphere. Low-pressure systems charge in from the west, absorb the heat, intensify and punish the lands to the east with storms and high winds.

For almost two centuries, the gleaming Great Lakes have beckoned people like magnets. In 1800, some 300,000 native North Americans and European immigrants lived next to their blue-green shorelines. The lakes gifted them with food, drinking water, and an irresistible highway. In time, a necklace of great cities—Milwaukee, Chicago, Detroit, Toledo, Cleveland, Buffalo, Toronto, Hamilton, and Rochester—grew up along their coasts. When the *Fitzgerald* was built, tens of millions of people, one-seventh of all United States citizens and one-fourth of all Canadians, were clustered next to their shores. A few visionaries were warning that there were too many people, that there was too much waste, and that the lakes were sorely stressed.

But for the shipowners, shipbuilders, and ship operators it wasn't the health of the lakes that mattered, it was the health of their businesses. They were in the highly competitive business of building ships and moving cargo. The lakes were a convenient corridor. In the *Fitzgerald* they had a ship that would steam through the roughest waters and remain as steady as a pier, her wide beam and audacious length trampling everything that nature laid before her. In the *Fitzgerald* they had conquest by size, the dream of every shipbuilder for thousands of years.

At 7:00 a.m. on Monday, September 22, 1958, Captain Bert Lambert eased his new ship out of its Rouge River berth and headed her north on her maiden voyage. Over the past five years he had been master of the

620-foot *Armco*, which, until the time of the *Fitzgerald*, was the flagship
of the Columbia line. A seaman since 1917 and a captain since 1939,
Lambert was endearingly modest. When asked by a reporter how it felt
to be the first captain of the largest ship on the lakes, he replied, "I
hardly know how to answer you. I guess it feels fine. I know it certainly
makes a fellow feel good when employers think you are doing a good
enough job to pick you for a better one."

Two days later, in foggy and wet weather, Captain Lambert steered
the *Fitzgerald* into the ore docks at Silver Bay, Minnesota, on the north
shore of Lake Superior to pick up a load of black taconite pellets. Friday
evening he sailed into Toledo, Ohio, and unloaded a record-breaking
cargo. The records would continue to be made until 1960, when a sister
ship, the *Arthur B. Homer*, slid down the ways. It was the beginning of a
competition that sparked arguments between lake sailors about which
was the better ship. In July of that year, the *Fitzgerald* broke her old
record with a 25,828-ton load and one month later increased it to
26,451 tons. Four days later, the *Homer* and her crew steamed out of
Silver Bay with a load that topped this by 551 tons.

In 1964, under the command of Captain N. C. Larsen, the *Fitzgerald*
became the first Great Lakes freighter to carry a million tons of ore
through the Soo Locks. In 1967, her new master, Captain Pete Pulcher,
achieved a long-sought record — 30,000 tons in a single trip. And he did
this not once, but four times: twice in July and twice in August.

Pulcher was an exuberant cigar-smoking skipper with a booming
voice and a reputation as considerable as his big red ship. When he
eased the *Fitz* into the Soo Locks on warm summer days, he would turn
up the volume of his public-address system and entertain guests on the
elevated observation deck with a running commentary on the *Fitzgerald*'s
dimensions, the weight of her cargo, her travel route, and her next port
of call. Most times he would have his officers turn out in their dress uniforms, but on one trip he showed his sense of humor when he and most
of the crew on deck wore Ronald McDonald fluorescent-orange wigs.
Sometimes, as he steamed slowly down the Detroit River, he turned up
the volume of his pilothouse speakers and played Mozart and Handel.
Summer vacationers returned home with stories of being woken up on a
Sunday morning by the sounds of "The Magic Flute" or "Water Music"
coming from a passing freighter.

During her 17 years of service, the *Fitzgerald* was involved in six collisions, or groundings. All six were officially listed as minor. On September 6, 1969, she ran aground at Sault Ste. Marie while approaching the locks. Later that year, she went into dry dock so that marine engineers and naval architects could inspect her hull. They found a series of cracks at the keelson-to-shell connections; the area was strengthened by welding steel stiffeners to both sides of the keelson.

In his 1992 book, *Edmund Fitzgerald 1957–1975*, Robert E. Lee of the Great Lakes Maritime Institute described the *Fitzgerald*'s other collisions and groundings:

- On April 30, 1970, she collided with the *Hochelaga*. Damages were to the J, K, L and M strakes, frames 117-165 (hatches 18 and 19).
- On September 4, 1970, she struck a lock wall at the Soo and suffered damage in L strake, frames 245-162 (hatches 18 and 19).
- The lock wall was hit again in May 1973, and on June 17, 1974. On each occasion similar damage was experienced.
- In September 1974, the crew inadvertently started to lift the cover from Number 8 hatch without removing all of the hatch clamps. Four clamps coamings, hatch covers and stiffeners were damaged.

Depending on the weather, the shipping season on the Great Lakes runs from about April to December. During January, February, and March, restless sheets of ice invade the lakes, sending even the most rugged vessels to seek shelter in big-city harbors. Each spring, as the Arctic released its grip, the *Fitzgerald* was spruced up and began her unvaried trek across the earth-curving arc of Lake Superior, down the length of Lake Huron, and into the western end of Lake Erie. And then she turned around and went back again. It was a five-day round trip she would repeat, in storm and fair weather, some 45 times every year.

It cost thousands of dollars a day to operate an eight-million-dollar ore carrier, and her owners were always looking for ways to improve her efficiency. In 1969, a diesel-powered bow thruster was installed. Located in the bow below the waterline, the thruster made the big ship more maneuverable. During the winter of 1971–72, the *Fitzgerald* was converted from coal to oil. The dusty black bunkers next to her boilers were replaced by two, large fuel oil tanks. Combustion and a feed-water control system were installed on her boilers.

Marine boilers use purified fresh water, circulated through a closed system of pipes. The furnace in the boilers heats this water to steam, which spins the turbines. The weakened steam is piped to condensers to be cooled back to water and returned to the boilers for another cycle. Cooling the condensers is achieved by drawing lake water into the ship, circulating it through an arrangement of pipes, and ejecting the heated water back into the lake. A breakdown in either of these two closed water systems will cause the boilers to fail.

It happens more frequently than shipowners like to admit. In April 1974, just as the *Fitzgerald* was beginning her sixteenth season of work, the *Queen Elizabeth II* was steaming across the Atlantic when oil started leaking into her distilled-water steam system. Southwest of Bermuda, the celebrity ship lost all power and drifted helplessly with 1,600 passengers on board.

Early in 1972, the command of the *Fitzgerald* was turned over to Captain Ernest McSorley. By that time she was no longer the most impressive ship on the lake. There were several other vessels of the same dimensions. But to her new captain and crew, the *Fitzgerald* was still the flagship of the fleet. She had a long history and a style in her lines that the newer vessels could not match. And she was still a substantial ship. When "summer loaded" she was only a few thousand tons lighter than the *Titanic*. By early November 1975, in her seventeenth year of service, she had logged some 748 voyages up and down the astonishing expanse of the Great Lakes. This meant that more than a million miles of water had passed beneath her keel, a distance roughly equivalent to 44 trips around the world.

Chapter Three

THE FIRST TWELVE HOURS

With a load of iron ore twenty-six thousand tons more than the Edmund
*   Fitzgerald weighed empty,*
That good ship and true was a bone to be chewed when the "Gales of
*   November" came early*

The day before November 9, 1975, over the high plains of west Texas, a mass of cold air from the mountain states drifted up against a mass of warm air from the Gulf of Mexico and formed a stationary front. Urged on by its own weight and the implacable turning of the planet, the cold air began to slide under the warm air, creating a bend or "wave" in the front. Rotating to the southeast, the cold air pushed a wedge of warm air to the northeast, setting in motion an anti-clockwise circulation of winds. That evening, forecasters in Chicago and Toronto penciled in a new low-pressure cell on their weather maps.

On Sunday morning, as the *Fitzgerald* was being loaded, the young weather system worked its way northeast across the flatlands of Kansas. The many layers of clouds that marked its progress were now miles long and growing outward like spiral nebula. Driven by the temperature difference of the colliding air masses and the overhead path of the jet stream, the system's internal winds began to increase. At 10:30 a.m., a National Weather Service forecaster in Chicago read the following bulletin: "On Lake Superior the winds will be out of the east...and increasing to 20 to 33 knots tonight." Five hours later, after looking at the computer printouts of millibars and isobars, the forecast was changed to read "and tonight the winds will be 34 to 38 knots."

For the *Fitzgerald* and her crew steaming at 16 knots across the western reach of the lake, it was just another cold November afternoon. The sun was still out, but low in the sky. The blue shorelines to the north and south were visible, but fading as the ship moved farther east. The winds were less than 10 knots. Inside the great ship, all manner of work was being done—work that had been going on every sailing day since the *Fitzgerald*'s first voyage 17 years earlier.

Whenever a sailor came off duty and felt in need of a pick-me-up, he made his way toward the stern and the mess hall. He walked through its open door into a bright fluorescent space, inhaled the warm smells, and said hello to whoever was sitting at a table or working behind a serving counter. Then he poured a steaming mug of coffee, helped himself to a wedge of cherry pie or chocolate cake, and sat down to talk.

Feeding the *Fitzgerald*'s 29 men four meals a day and cleaning up afterward was an endless task that required two cooks, two porters, and an array of freezers, cupboards, counters, and two Garland gas stoves working overtime. The man in charge of this suite of stainless steel, with its rows of pots and pans and measuring cups, was 62-year-old Bob Rafferty. Rafferty wore a stained white apron and a rumpled white cook's hat that hid his large bald head. He weighed 200 pounds and moved from stove to refrigerator and back again with a heavy-footed grace, crafting his own special magic on soups and stews, bread and cakes. When he sensed storm waves beginning to play with his end of the ship, he slid a series of steel-retaining rods around the perimeter of his stoves and turned down the blue flames simmering under his stockpots.

Rafferty had spent half his life sweltering in the galleys of big ships, sailing in short voyages and long voyages and some that took him to the Far East and the South China Sea. He had steamed around the watery rim of the planet seven times and he was tired of missing his daughter, Pamela, his son, Randy, and his wife, Brooksie. Rafferty was getting ready to retire in Toledo, Ohio. To prepare for this, he began signing on as a temporary cook. A month earlier, when the *Fitz*'s chief cook, Dick Bishop, had fallen sick, Rafferty had gladly accepted an offer to replace him. It was mid-November and the season was almost over.

✝

It was getting dark when the men in the *Fitzgerald*'s pilothouse first sighted the Apostle Islands off to starboard. There were 22 islands and, even in the twilight, their low, dark, heavily forested shapes looked like walls breached by the lake. Scattered between them were ship-wrecking shoals. The slim beams of their eight lighthouses — the greatest concentration of lighthouses in the Great Lakes — pierced the onrushing night.

To the north of the *Fitzgerald*'s trackline lay the Minnesota shore, which ran from the southwest corner of Lake Superior to the Canadian border. It was a forbidding coastline with pounding surf and high black cliffs brooded over by the spiked peaks of the Sawteeth Mountains. The long straight coast had no sheltering islands. There were many days and nights when it was obscured by fog.

The port of Two Harbors was built around one of the few sanctuaries that nature had created along the northern shore. At 4:30 p.m., a ship slightly bigger than the *Fitzgerald* and also loaded with iron ore eased past the stone breakwall at Two Harbors and headed out into the open lake. She was the *Arthur M. Anderson*, a 767-foot ore carrier operated by U.S. Steel. Her captain was Bernie Cooper, a stocky man with more than 30 years of experience on the lakes. Captain Cooper was about to become the main witness to the events that would unfold during the next 36 hours. The quotations that follow are drawn from his recollection of those events.

> *"When we left Two Harbors that afternoon, on the 9th, it was one of those really special days on Lake Superior. It was warm, ripples on the water. It was a beautiful, clear November day. As we backed out of Two Harbors, we could see the* Fitzgerald *on the horizon. We knew it was the* Fitzgerald *because we heard her security report coming out of Superior ..."*

The *Anderson* was bound for the steel mills at Gary, Indiana, and so the two vessels proceeded eastward on parallel, then converging, courses, separated by about 12 miles.

The center of the storm moving toward Michigan and the open waters of Superior was by now an extra-tropical cyclone, an enormous rotating wheel of lurid gray clouds in layers, furrows, and towers. At its highest levels, within reach of the rarefied air of the stratosphere, the cyclone was pulling down winds, pressing them earthward. On the high western fringes of the storm, the sun diminished. A swarm of stars came out, flickered briefly on the edge of the earth, and vanished.

The increasing winds blowing across Lake Superior created a series of waves that grew in height and volume. The waves had the same bleak profile as the Sawteeth Mountains to the north. When the wind pressed into their backs, it broke the summit water into white foam, reformed it into bigger waves, and broke them again. It was a cadence almost as old as the planet, a message sent from the sun.

> *"... After we were on the lake a couple of hours, the weather people put out small craft warnings.... Whenever the weather people become a little bit nervous, I do too.... But I don't always go along with what they say.... That evening it didn't look like anything that was really out of the ordinary, might be a fresh gale or something, nothing for these particular ships...."*

Both vessels continued to steam east across the immense lake. No stars or moon lit their way. The points of light coming from their bows and sterns gleamed feebly, giving no hint of the exacting toil and discipline under way in the pilothouse, engine room, and other parts of the ship.

To keep the *Fitzgerald* operating 24 hours a day, the men were divided into three watches reporting to Captain McSorley. Each of the ship's three officers were responsible for one watch: first mate Jack McCarthy, who, in addition to supervising the loading and unloading, oversaw all the work on deck and stood day and night watches in the pilothouse; second mate James Pratt, in charge of the ship's charts, technical publications, and compliance with government regulations; and third mate Michael Armagost, responsible for safety, fire-fighting equipment, emergency drills, and many other duties.

"Big Mike" Armagost was more than six feet tall, weighed 230 pounds, and had a generous woodsman's beard. He was 37 years old and lived in Iron River, Wisconsin. When he wasn't sailing the Great Lakes, he was out in the bush hunting for deer, fishing for pickerel, or racing snowmobiles through cold winter nights. Armagost was intense, offbeat, and original. One cool April night, years earlier in Iron River, he poured back a few, saddled his sister's horse, and guided it carefully up the steps and through the front door of Billy's Bar. The music stopped; the crowd grew silent. The horse's head reared and, with flawless exhilaration, Big Mike fired off a few yelps and rode out through the back door.

Born in 1938 to Lorraine and Kendall Armagost and raised in the woods of northern Wisconsin, Big Mike was 19 years old when his father died. A few weeks after the funeral, he went down to the docks and took a job as a deckhand on a Great Lakes ship. Each month he sent part of his paycheck to his widowed mother.

Big Mike liked the challenge of the work. And he liked the lakes; their measureless spaces and accidental beauties reminded him of the northern woods. And he was happy with the men. They could be maddening, bullheaded, and unreadable, but like him, they were all gypsy-blooded.

Big Mike also liked the freedom of the long winter months, when he could do what he damn well pleased. Deer hunting. Ice fishing. Watching Vince Lombardi's Green Bay Packers fight their way to two consecutive Super Bowl championships. Or dreaming of owning a big pine-timbered resort lodge on a secluded Wisconsin lake.

In 1960, he took a job on a Liberian freighter sailing out of New Orleans. His first ocean voyage took him down the Gulf of Mexico, across the South Atlantic around the Cape of Good Hope, and into the Indian Ocean. It was an interesting journey but it took too long and kept him away from the Wisconsin woods. He never went back to the great salt ocean again.

Big Mike was the kind of man who read books and thought hard about things. Why some ships were good ships and others were bad. Why some captains had innate resolve and others had unresolved insecurities. Why there was magic in blue-green shorelines that appeared and disappeared. Like most of his shipmates, Big Mike had fallen under the spell described by novelist Joseph Conrad: "Nothing is more enticing, disenchanting, enslaving than life at sea..."

In 1962, Big Mike enlisted in the army and spent two years at Fort Carsen, Colorado. The mountains were exhilarating and the drill grounds of the Red Diamond Division increased his sense of trust and responsibility, but he missed the life on the lakes. So he went back to the ships.

In 1964, Big Mike Armagost signed up with Columbia Transportation and in turn served on the *Ben E. Tate*, the *Ashland*, and the *Reserve*. Whenever he climbed up the slanting steel gangway of a new ship, his duffel bag was heavy with books. Among his favorites were western novels like *Shane* and *Gunsmoke*. As the seasons passed and his experience increased, he decided that he had what it took to be an officer. He began adding books on navigation and ship handling to the small library in his room.

In 1967, while working on the main deck, Armagost slipped on a taconite pellet and injured his back. The ship's captain told him to take two weeks off. It was August. Armagost figured that the best way to recover was to return to Iron River and go fishing with his buddies. He spent the long, hot days fishing in the nearby streams and creeks with a couple of school chums, his big dog Mack, and a case of water-cooled beer. On one especially hot night they drove over to the Norseman Lodge, went into the taproom, and paused to let their eyes adjust to the dim light. Big Mike scanned the room until his eyes came to rest on the attractive face and figure of a University of Wisconsin coed. Before he knew what was happening, he was heading toward her.

Janice Doyle looked up to see him coming. The room filled with a tall, powerfully built young man who had wavy brown hair and piercing blue eyes. Four months later they were engaged.

On October 5, 1969, they were married in the Catholic church in Monona, Wisconsin. They spent their honeymoon in a small log cabin nestled in the pine trees. In time they had a daughter, Michele. Three years later, they had a son, Christopher Michael. Big Mike thought of them often, especially at night on the lakes. They were the center of his life.

"We were proceeding east under worsening conditions. At about nine o'clock the weather people put out gale warnings, which is 32 to 38 knots.... This is nothing much when you have seas running maybe ten feet.... And it was really no problem. But Captain McSorley and myself, we talked the situation over and figured as we proceeded east across the lake, we would heave up under Isle Royale and try to get what lee we could from the land..."

Isle Royale is the largest island in Lake Superior. Its 90-mile length and abrupt cliffs offer a good refuge from a northeasterly gale. About an hour after midnight, the *Fitzgerald* was running parallel to the island at a distance of about 20 miles. Her faster speed had allowed her to almost overtake the *Anderson*. At this time, the officer on watch in the *Fitzgerald* pilothouse called in a weather report to the station in Marquette, Michigan, reporting "Winds from the northeast at 52 knots with an overcast sky and visibility two to five miles in continuous heavy rain." Outside the pilothouse the temperature was five degrees above freezing. The officer described the waves as being "10 feet high."

Even in a good light it's hard to judge the height of waves when standing in a pilothouse looking down through a wet window toward the ship's bow. At night, it's even harder. And, as every mariner knows, all storm waves are not created equal. Some of the waves breaking against the *Fitzgerald*'s hull were 10 feet high and some were smaller. But some of the waves that broke over the ship's main deck were certainly much bigger.

Chapter Four

THE SECOND TWELVE HOURS

The wind in the wires made a tattletale sound and a wave broke over the
railing
And ev'ry man knew as the captain did too 'twas the witch of November
come stealin'

Sometime after two o'clock in the morning of November 10, Captain
Cooper walked across the slanting deck of the *Anderson*'s pilothouse,
reached for his VHF radio, and called Captain McSorley. Cooper had
just heard a weather forecast calling for northeast winds of 50 knots.
The master of the *Anderson* had always worked hard at meteorology and
he knew that this was an average estimated speed and that the gusts
inside these winds might be considerably higher. During their conversation, both captains expressed concern about the deteriorating weather.
Their ships were moving across an unlighted wilderness and being
mauled by waves with breaking crests. These waves did not have the
slower cadence and round peaks of ocean waves. They came in fast and
sharp, angled with the weight of a slab of marble. They punched under a
ship's bow, lifting it and then dropping it abruptly. When these waves
hit, water went everywhere, unchecked, flying out from under the hull,
arcing upward, pounding against the pilothouse windows.

McSorley agreed that it would be prudent to depart from the normal
shipping lanes near the south shore of the lake and proceed on a more
northerly course. A few more hours of steaming would bring both ships
into the lee of the Canadian shore.

At three o'clock that same morning, the duty officer on the *Anderson*
called for a course change to 55 degrees. The wind-speed indicator on
the forward wall of the pilothouse was reading a steady 42 knots. The
officer noted that the wind was gusting over the port side at approximately 21 degrees from the point of the bow. He also saw that the

Fitzgerald, because of her faster speed, was slowly pulling ahead of the *Anderson*.

Located under the *Fitzgerald*'s stern smokestack was her engine room, an all-steel atrium nearly three stories high and built around the massive main propulsion turbine, the feed pumps, the feed manifold, the main condensers, and the side by side high-pressure boilers. The hot, white-painted room was designed so that its catwalks, ladders, and stairwells gave an unobstructed view of the constantly working machinery and hundreds of pipes, shafts, valves, meters, and gauges. The engine room was windowless, well lighted, and filled with deafening noise. Its lowest deck, which held the heaviest of the engines, lay 10 feet below the *Fitzgerald*'s waterline.

In a storm, the engine room was the most stable part of the ship. The placement of the cargo, the position of the propeller, and the weight of the main turbine gave it a majestic immutability. It was a fluorescent world inhabited by engineers and oilers, a gang of men in grease-stained cotton coveralls who toiled with profound concentration among thousands of fiercely moving parts. They were men whose hearing was diminished from standing for hours beside engines that roared. There were three oilers — Bentsen, Wilhelm, and Walton — and a wiper, MacLellan, working four-hour shifts in the engine room. They were apprentices who assisted the engineers by oiling and greasing the machinery, shifting equipment and stores, and keeping the engine room clean.

The lord of the room was the chief engineer, George J. Holl, a man who could listen and know exactly where to squirt a few drops of oil in the front end of the turbogenerator. Like Captain McSorley up in the bow, Holl was on call 24 hours a day. Working under him was Ed Bindson, the first assistant engineer. Bindson was the official manager of the engine room; each morning he pinned the work schedule on the bulletin board and assigned tasks to everyone. Just below him in rank was Tom Edwards, the second engineer. Edward's many responsibilities included boiler-water purity, oil sampling and testing, and safety equipment and drills.

Among the hazards of working in the aft end of the ship were fire and flooding. For every man who worked here, the discipline of prevention was part of every routine and procedure. It was a discipline supported by self-reliance, a reverence for machinery, and a sense of humor.

These traits definitely resided in the tall, muscular frame of Oliver Joseph "Buck" Champeau. The third assistant engineer was 41 years old and had coal-black hair, a bushy mustache, and the soul of a Salvation Army minister. Champeau had been riding the ships since 1961, when he got his first job on a Milwaukee car ferry. His father had been a master mechanic who could disassemble an engine on Saturday and have it purring on Sunday. When he died, Buck Champeau's world collapsed. Thirteen years old and the eldest of five children, he had looked on in disbelief as his father's car and five-drawer toolbox were sold to pay for the funeral. For the next two years, Buck's mother took in washing and cleaned houses to support her three sons and two daughters. One morning, looking into her exhausted eyes, Buck decided to quit school. Soon after, he went to work driving a coal truck. During the Korean War, he served in the Marines, on board the *USS Oriskinay*. He watched helplessly as his friends were killed and injured. Back at home, he developed an empathy for those who had little or nothing at all. He befriended derelicts, bringing them food and sometimes bringing them home. He became a smiling fixture at the local rescue mission.

Buck Champeau, who had been working in the *Fitzgerald*'s engine room for three years, knew the throttle-control levers and automatic combustion and feedwater systems as well as he knew Wisconsin's backwoods. He had his second-assistant engineering papers, but on this trip he was sailing as third. A year ago he had purchased a waterfront lot on Sturgeon Bay and was building a cottage. The extra income from this trip would pay off the loan for the lot he had purchased with his brothers Jack and Tom.

At 4:00 a.m., the watch was changed in the ship's engine room and bridge. The *Fitzgerald* was now shouldering her way east toward the Canadian shore, surrounded by glistening waves whose dark, broken ridges succeeded each other endlessly, their crests rising and falling in the blackness. There was a continuous din, the deep churning of the wind, toppling waves, the boom of water against steel, the hard staccato of spray falling in sheets on a long, open deck.

The men coming off the midwatch made their way down the stairways and passageways to their rooms. Measuring the next deep roll of the ship, they opened doors, clicked on overhead lights, and saw the flash of soothing colors on the four walls they called home. They paused for a moment between the small writing desk, the bed, and the porthole with the slab of round steel bolted behind it, wondering what to do next. They fussed. They brushed their teeth, leafed through newspapers, or shaved. A few, still in their soiled clothes, turned off the light, lay down, positioned themselves to counter the ship's motion, and fell asleep. Most of them turned on the bed light and tried to read or just lay there listening to the portentous din outside the hull.

"Sleep," according to the 16th-century poet Sydney Philip, "is the poor man's warmth, the prisoner's release." But most of them did not sleep. Standing four-hour watches, day after day, night after night, week after week, meant they were among the professionally sleep-deprived. Long hours of restful slumber had to be compressed into short, dreamless naps. Fatigue was an old friend. At times, unable to nap, they lay there and tried to think of something else. The long, boring shipping season that had passed. The sweetness of winter's freedom that would be theirs after one or two more voyages; the delights and despair waiting for them at home.

To ease their loneliness, their thoughts drifted to women, like those ideal women, undressed and airbrushed, in the photographs that adorned their closets and work spaces. They had an extravagant affection for these women, who demanded nothing yet answered all their wishes.

The big ship plunged forward, pursuing its way blindly across the northeast reach of the lake. The sky was starless; inside the hush of the pilothouse, a small group of men listened to the heavy rain. On this night they were excessively vigilant. Another ship—without power and without lights—could be lying ahead of them in the blackness. She might be a cargo ship or fishing boat unable to use her engine or radio. To the south of the *Fitzgerald*'s heading was a pinnacle of rock that shot up from 150 fathoms until it was only three fathoms below the surface.

There was not much that needed to be said by the three, and sometimes four, men standing watch. Binoculars were raised, the radar was scanned, and on a dimly lit table behind the helmsman, one of the men leaned over a chart with pencil and protractors, constantly plotting the *Fitzgerald*'s position. Occasionally, due to the set of the wind and the waves, a slight change of heading was required. A command was given by the officer of the watch and repeated by the wheelsman. Sometimes the captain repeated it too.

Like all the sailors who crossed Lake Superior, these men occasionally thought about the temperature of the water. It was only a few degrees above freezing. If you fell into it, the cold would be so intense it would feel like a kick in the stomach. You would live for about 30 minutes before the cold sucked the life out of you. The only value of your life jacket would be to help the searchers find your body.

One of the few men on board the *Fitzgerald* who did not swim was watchman Ray Ransom Cundy. Cundy looked very much the way you would expect an old-time watchman to look. Fifty-three years old, he dressed in battered boots, faded jeans, and thermal undershirts with faded work shirts over them. When he worked on deck he climbed into a weathered set of coveralls. His walk was loose and gangly, timed to the roll of the ship. When he stopped to talk to you, he tugged at his dark blue baseball cap, lit up a cigarette, and smiled.

Ray Cundy grew up in Houghton, Michigan, a mining town on the south shore of Lake Superior. Years ago, Houghton had been part of the mythical mid-century America, where everything seemed possible. Today, on its gritty streets, life was a constant struggle. When he was in his early twenties, Cundy was drawn to the big ships that sailed across Lake Superior. With the exception of a two-year tour in the Merchant Marine during the Second World War, he had spent his entire working life on the big freighters. Over the years, he had been a deckhand and watchman on the *Armco*, the *Reserve*, and the *Davidson*. For the previous six years, he had been on the *Fitzgerald*. He liked the big ships, but 30 years was more than enough. Ray had informed his friends and family that he was going to retire after this season.

One reason Ray Cundy wore a baseball cap was that he was as bald as Friar Tuck. His mates called him "skin-head" or "handsome Ransom," but he just smiled. Fate had given him an ironclad, rustproof sense of humor. His wisecracks and practical jokes made him one of the most popular men on the *Fitzgerald*.

In the summer of 1968, Ray Cundy was working on board the *Davidson* during a stopover near Buffalo, New York. While he was helping unload cargo, he looked across the dark water to the ship in the next berth. She was the *Lonson*, a black-hulled veteran of Canada's Algoma

Line. Standing on her stern was an attractive brunette in a white cook's uniform. He waved. To his surprise, she lifted her arm and waved back.

The following night he walked down the dock, across the street, and into a nearby tavern. Some of his shipmates were already there, filling the room with laughter. Later, as they sat exchanging gossip and opinions, the door opened and a dark-haired woman in a pretty dress came in with two other women. It was the cook from the *Lonson*. Cundy pushed back his chair, made his way across the room, and introduced himself.

Her name was Doreen. She lived in Canada and had a nine-year-old daughter, Dorlean, by a previous marriage. Cundy had two daughters, Jeanette and Cheryl, by a previous marriage. Cundy and Doreen talked for a long time. Later that night they returned to their ships, aware that something special had taken place. Shortly after, they began the nine-month exchange of letters that would lead to their marriage.

Having worked on board a freighter, Doreen was the ideal sailor's wife. She accepted Ray's long absences from their home in Superior, Wisconsin, and celebrated the times he was home. As the years passed, his eldest daughter, Jeanette, made him a grandfather not once, but twice. It was something he loved telling the boys on the boat.

One day, in 1974, Ray Ransom Cundy woke up to discover how unkind the world could be. Sometime during the night before, his son-in-law had shot and killed his beloved Jeanette before putting a bullet through his own head. In less time than it takes to pass through the Soo Locks, Ray Cundy became a different man. Paralyzed with grief, he began drinking.

It would take more than a year for him to work through his suffering. Slowly, Ray Cundy learned to draw strength from the emotional support offered by his family and friends. He eased the pain by approaching each day with humility and faith. He worked hard on recapturing his sense of humor. He rediscovered laughter.

"As we proceeded across the lake we were still moving pretty well up to the north, in fact the Fitzgerald *was quite a bit further to the north than I was. About six o'clock in the morning we got another weather report, and you could see the storm was starting to contract. In other words it was getting smaller and more intense... it showed northeast winds... gale force winds... and we proceeded east."*

At 7:00 a.m., the center of the storm was located on the south shore of Lake Superior, over the town of Marquette, Michigan. The multiple layers of clouds circulating around the center had expanded to cover Lakes Superior, Michigan, Huron, and most of Lakes Erie and Ontario. To the east, a huge dome of high pressure, stretching from Baffin Island to Nova Scotia began to increase the velocity of the the high-altitude winds. To the west, an enormous mass of polar air was accelerating southeastward. As the storm moved over the roiling expanse of Lake Superior, it drew the summer's heat from the water and increased its fury.

At 10:30 a.m., the National Weather Service office in Chicago revised the forecast for eastern Lake Superior. The movement of the center across the lake meant that the direction of the winds would be shifting rapidly from east to west: "North to northwest winds 32 to 48 knots this afternoon becoming northwesterly 25 to 48 knots tonight...waves 8 to 16 feet..."

The storm's center crossed Lake Superior to the west of Michipicoten Island. In the wake of its passing, a ragged line of roaring winds shifted from the northeast to the northwest, driving the surface of the lake in the opposite direction.

By mid-morning, both ships had struggled to within 25 miles of the Canadian shore. The *Fitzgerald*, still ahead of the *Anderson*, approached the shore and then turned south. The barometers in both pilothouses had fallen sharply. Fifty-knot winds were shredding the tops of the endless rows of steep-sided waves.

When a big ship is sailing through a gale, she rises, falls, rolls, and yaws, responding to the forces transmitted through the water. There are sounds and motions and full-length shudders that do not occur in good weather. All through the morning both Cooper and McSorley felt the quickening within their ships. There was no cause for alarm, only an increased attentiveness, part of the continual dialogue between the man in command and the vessel he was responsible for.

Chapter Five

THE LAST FIVE HOURS

*The dawn came late and the breakfast had to wait when the gale of
November came slashin'*

At midday on November 10, the storm had some of the hallmarks of a
tropical hurricane. Its wild, gray, corrugated center was some 20 miles
wide. Inside this aqueous eye, down near the surface of the lake, the
winds were relatively calm. The highest winds and the densest clouds
were inside the rotating wall of clouds. High overhead was a shadowy
universe of altostratus and cirrostratus and, somewhere above that, a
pale November sun.

*"... a little after noon we went through the eye of the storm. This type of
storm was essentially a hurricane.... On the back side of the low the winds are
never as great as they are on the northeastern quadrant.... The concentration
seems to be tighter on the northeast side of the storm, which is where we went,
unfortunately."*

At approximately 1:40 p.m., Cooper told McSorley that he anticipated
the wind was going to shift into the northwest. He added that, to keep
the seas on his stern, he intended to change course to the west before
passing Michipicoten Island. Seventeen miles long, this high, densely
wooded island lies only 10 miles from the mainland. Several ships,
including the freighters *Chicago* and *Strathmore*, have been claimed by its
shoals. Captain McSorley, whose vessel was just past the western end of
the island, indicated that he would continue on his course, although the
Fitzgerald was "rolling some."

Ten minutes later, with the *Fitzgerald* some three miles ahead and about three miles off the west end of Michipicoten, Captain Cooper brought his ship around to 230 degrees, a more westerly heading. The winds had dropped to five knots. The visibility was fair.

"We passed through the eye of the storm. Unbelievable. The sun was out. Good weather. The Fitzgerald *was still way up to the north of me and I thought 'Why beat about the bush?' I headed up the lee of Michipicoten and about half an hour later, so did the* Fitzgerald. *When the* Fitzgerald *passed off the west end of Michipicoten she was…about seventeen miles ahead of me. After she passed…the weather changed dramatically. There was a slow southwest flow running on the front side of the low. Then the* Fitzgerald *disappeared from sight. Snow, blinding snow, came down…"*

One of the most important reference books in a ship's library is the *American Practical Navigator*, published by the U.S. Navy Hydrographic Office. The 1,500-page hardcover volume known as the Bible of Navigation was first published by Nathaniel Bowditch in 1802. In its description of hurricanes, it states: "As the wall on the opposite side of the eye arrives, the full fury of the wind strikes as suddenly as it ceased, but from the opposite direction." Within minutes the winds rose from near calm to 50 knots, creating a chaos of colliding energies. In less time than it took the *Fitzgerald* to traverse three leagues, the waves striking its starboard side were as high as houses.

Bowditch warns: "The wind increases. The seas become mountainous. The tops of huge waves are blown off and fill the air with water. Objects at a short distance are not visible. Even the largest and most seaworthy vessels…may sustain heavy damage. Less sturdy vessels do not survive. Navigation virtually stops as safety of the vessel becomes the primary consideration. The awesome fury of this condition can only be experienced. Words are inadequate to describe it."

Deep inside this fury, the *Fitzgerald*'s hull flexed majestically. It was designed to bend. Its builders knew there would be times when the hull would be held by big waves at both ends or by a massive wave under its center. But there were limits to this pliability. It was one of the reasons why the big ships were loaded so carefully. In addition, if the weight of the cargo was not distributed evenly, the forces of gravity worked against the forces of buoyancy and created stress fractures in the steel. These were tiny cracks shaped like lightning bolts that could threaten the integrity of the hull.

During its next broadcast, the National Weather Service in Chicago revised the forecast for eastern Lake Superior. It now predicted "Northwest winds 38 to 52 knots with gusts up to 60 knots early tonight...."

For 17 years, the hull of the *Edmund Fitzgerald* had been exposed to constantly moving streams of air and water. Like all steel ships, her hull plates were vulnerable to an insidious chemical process in which oxygen and water combined with iron to form rust. The reddish-brown crust was brittle and flaked off, continuously exposing a fresh surface. Although slower in fresh water, it is a process that eats away at steel with unceasing intensity. The buckling strength of a steel plate is directly related to its thickness; if a plate's thickness is reduced by a third, its resistance to buckling may be reduced by 50 percent.

At 2:45 p.m., under a rapidly darkening sky, the *Anderson*'s heading was changed to 131 degrees. Like the *Fitzgerald* in the mist up ahead, she was fighting the furious sideway forces of wind and waves. As the two ships listed to one side, their decks were inundated with raging water. Deep beneath their keels ran a network of submerged fissures and plateaus. One of the fissures to the west held the lake's maximum depth of 1,333 feet. But ahead, in much shallower water, lay a monster mesa with high escarpments.

The mesa held the only two large islands—Michipicoten and Caribou—in the eastern end of the lake. The radars of both ships confirmed they were heading southeast between them. What the radars could not show was a wide rostrum of rock, known as Six Fathom Shoal, extending out from one of the islands.

Although Six Fathom Shoal was marked on the chart, its printed contours were inaccurate. It ran for about a mile farther north than indicated. The men in the *Fitzgerald*'s pilothouse had no idea if the lake bed was rising beneath them because, despite the full suite of nautical technology she boasted, the *Fitzgerald* did not carry a fathometer. All they knew was that their ship was sailing between blinding sky and water.

The lake roared past her bows. Her forepeak shuddered and made clangorous sounds. Waves with snowy crests rose behind her, filling the air with thundering octaves, lifting her, lowering her, impelling her southward. In her engine room and pilothouse, in the galley and other rooms where the men had gathered in small groups, there was a sense of siege. Every room, every corridor, every workplace was charged with an oppressive atmosphere. Life still seemed an indestructible thing, but as the ship rose and fell and then rose again, as if trying to shrug off the fury of the lake, the men looked at each other, sobered by their reliance on the invisible.

The *Fitzgerald*'s southward course past Caribou Island carried the ship into the heart of the culminating gale. With increasing regularity, green water broke over the deck, submerging the lifelines, choking the scuppers, trying to gain entry into the hatches. When a bigger wave broke across the long deck, the forward and after deckhouses were like islands in a turbulent sea.

The pilothouse had become a self-contained outpost where men studied their instruments in the dim light and, with heightened awareness, peered through water-drenched windows at a darkling sea. For years they had measured their strength and experience against the rages of the lakes. They had seen accidents and injuries and storms, but nothing like this. Until now, they had never given much thought to what the great waters might do.

It was getting darker. There was no sun, no sky, no stars — nothing but furious winds and a wilderness of water. The men could not remember such waves or such winds. But their job was to keep her boilers fired and her head pointed in the right direction, and they did. Working away at their stations, they forgot the land, they forgot the sunshine, and they forgot the day of the week. In the younger men there was a sense of pride at being able to struggle through such a trial. In the older men there was a sense of foreboding.

At 3:20 p.m., the *Anderson* was seven miles off the west end of Michipicoten Island — the *Fitzgerald* was some 15 miles ahead. The lake was closing its grip on both ships. The winds were raging out of the northwest at a steady 43 knots. Intermittently, the ships passed through black squalls bearing snow and sleet. The seas were averaging 16 feet in height and both vessels were shipping tons of water across their decks.

Captain Cooper tried to keep the *Anderson* on a heading of 125 degrees, a course he believed would keep them well clear of Six Fathom Shoal. The sky was low and gray. The *Fitzgerald* was a shade to the right of dead ahead. As the ships struggled forward, the men in the *Anderson*'s pilothouse saw the *Fitzgerald* pass north and east of Caribou Island. Cooper turned to his first mate and told him that the *Fitzgerald* had gone in too close to Six Fathom Shoal, closer than he wanted the *Anderson* to be.

At 3:35 p.m., McSorley called Cooper. In a brief conversation overheard by the *Anderson*'s first and second mates, McSorley told Cooper that his ship had been damaged. A fence rail was down, two ballast tank vents were lost, and his ship had a list. Captain Cooper asked Captain McSorley if he had "his pumps going " and the reply was "Yes, both of them."

As the two men talked, water was coming into the *Fitzgerald* from somewhere, through some imperceptible crevice or opening, pressing toward the center of the ship, urged by the weight of the lake behind it. At first it was as transparent as a mountain spring, but as it streamed and threaded its way along the insides of the steel plates it became dark and greasy. Slowly the water began to work its way forward and sternward, running beneath the vibrating caves that held the cargo. It was clear that if water was coming in, air was going out. The *Fitzgerald* was losing buoyancy.

> "He called me up and said 'I've got problems... I've got some vents torn off ... and... I've got a bad list.' And I said, 'Have you got your pumps going?' and he said 'Yeah.' And he said, 'Will you shadow me down the lake? I'll reduce my speed so that you can overtake me.' I said, 'Okay, we will do our best.' He must have reduced his speed about two miles an hour because our radar showed that we were picking up. From that time on we never saw the Fitzgerald. We had them on radar and we were plotting them, but we never saw them again because of the snow.
>
> "At 3:30 in the afternoon... their ship received a critical wound... She either grounded on an unknown shoal or... had a stress crack in her hull... and water poured into her faster than the pumps could take it out."

Invisibly, water continued to invade the *Fitzgerald*. It slid in, creating a deepening network of submerged eddies and currents. It flowed onward, hesitating only when it met a bulkhead or a stringer, slowly submerging the bottom steel frames and the lower reaches of the cargo. Never, for a moment, did it cease. Outside the steel shell of the ship, the surface of the lake churned violently; inside it was silent, like a tide, rising without check.

At 4:30 in the afternoon, dusk fell, obscuring the old and mysterious lake and the two ships trailing each other across its tortured surface. At 4:52 p.m., the *Anderson* drew abeam of the north end of Caribou Island and changed her course to 141 degrees. Like the *Fitzgerald*, fighting for her life in the snow ahead, the *Anderson* was steering south toward the sanctuary of Whitefish Bay. The seas were 16 feet and higher and breaking over her starboard side. Winds were measured at 58 knots.

"I think we had gusts of wind at over 100 miles an hour on a few occasions, but it was a constant sixty knots.... And when we got into the lee of Caribou, probably about 6:30 in the evening ... we took two of the largest seas we had taken on the whole trip.... Seas don't always run 35 feet, but these were two of the biggest. Normally they were sixteen to twenty-six feet and we could handle that ...

"...I had a hatch crane on deck. It stood about twelve feet above our deck and a couple of those seas that came across buried my entire deck in about twelve feet of water ... that old girl the Anderson, *she came out shaking like a dog.... Shaking water off, water flying all over ... I never gave it a thought. We had a good ship under us. But the* Fitzgerald... *was crippled and probably sinking for the three and a half hours after she called me ... water was seeping from the side tanks into the cargo, gradually pushing her bow ... one degree of list on that ship is equivalent to two and a half feet. It would put the starboard side down two and a half feet and bring the other side up two and a half feet ...*

"The winds and the seas were coming from just off her starboard quarter. So not only does she have a problem with structural damage, she's got a problem with the sea piling on her...

"Well, sometime after 6:30, these two huge waves came by and one of them flooded out my poop deck where my lifeboat was ... The chief engineer's wife was standing in the window looking forward. The deck just disappeared ... it's approximately 30 feet above the waterline, so these two seas had to be approximately 30 to 35 feet high. The water dropped down on top of the lifeboat ... then we took one wave on the bridge deck. The bridge deck is almost 35 feet above the water. Those seas were running by us about 12 to 15 miles an hour, passing us on the starboard side. If you figure that the

Fitzgerald was probably ten miles ahead of us and, at 15 miles an hour how far those seas were going to travel...I don't know, but I've often wondered if these two seas might have been the ones..."

The *Fitzgerald* pitched slowly forward as if diving into the lake, and then rammed into a wall of water. She lunged sideways, reeling under torrents of frothing water that boiled up, raced across her sloping deck, streamed through her wire railings, and poured off into the blackness of the night. At some point, the rotating radar antennae fixed to the roof of the pilothouse were torn from their brackets and melted away unseen and unheard.

The terrible power of a hurricane-force storm attacks a man like it attacks his ship, with mindless violence, trying to rout his courage. Each man knew that if the turbines did not give up, if the boilers did not fail, if the steering gear did not give way, or if the ship did not bury herself in one of those awful seas with the white crests toppling above her bow, there was a chance they would come through it. The protection of Whitefish Bay was only a little more than an hour away.

Like the other men in the pilothouse, Captain McSorley stood facing south, his lips compressed, his whole body braced against the next unpredictable lurch. The water pelting the pilothouse windows sounded like a hail of buckshot. McSorley knew the *Fitzgerald* from stem to stern, from her keel to the white light at the tip of her foremast. But on this night there was an unfamiliar feeling beneath his feet.

Chapter Six

THE FINAL MINUTES

Does anyone know where the love of God goes when the waves turn the minutes to hours?

After losing her radar, the *Fitzgerald* completely depended on the *Anderson* to aim her through the night into Whitefish Bay. At 7:00 p.m., the *Anderson* informed the *Fitzgerald* that they were "about 10 miles ahead and two miles to the left" of the *Anderson*'s heading, putting them about 15 miles from the highlands at Crisp Point. At 7:10, the mate on the *Anderson* called again and said: "There is a target 19 miles ahead of us, so the target is nine miles on ahead."

The *Fitzgerald* asked, "Well, am I going to clear?"

"Yes, he is going to pass to the west of you," the mate said.

The *Fitzgerald* replied, "Well, fine."

As the mate was about to sign off, he asked, "Oh, by the way, how are you making out with your problems?"

"We are holding our own," the *Fitzgerald* replied.

The winds were now shrieking across 200 miles of open lake, hurling hundreds of tons of water against the *Fitzgerald*'s listing deck. This particular convergence of forces was not what the marine architects had in mind when they'd crouched over their drawing boards 18 years earlier. And this night of terror, aboard a wounded ship, was not what the *Fitzgerald*'s men had anticipated when they signed on to become lake sailors. The threat of annihilation honed their senses and concentrated their minds. They stayed close to each other, for comfort, in the pilot-house, in the engine room, and in the galley. Their mouths were dry; their skin, cold. They spoke quietly to each other, fearing that the wrong word or the wrong intonation might reveal panic.

Joseph Conrad described it this way: "There are many shades in the danger of adventures and gales.... It is only now and then that there appears on the face of the facts a sinister violence of intention — that indefinable something which forces it upon the mind and heart of a man that...these elemental furies are coming at him with a purpose of malice, with a strength beyond control, with an unbridled cruelty that means to tear out of him his hope and his fear, the pain of his fatigue and his longing for rest, which means to smash, to destroy, to annihilate all he has seen, known, loved, enjoyed or hated, all that is priceless and necessary — the sunshine, the memories, the future — which means to sweep the whole precious world away from his sight by the simple and appalling act of taking his life..."

It happened without warning and without mercy. The big steel ship, burdened beyond buoyancy by water in her belly and water on her back, pitched forward into the trough of Lake Superior, buried her head, and never recovered. She shook violently, quivering from one end of her keel to the other, fighting the pull of gravity, but the lake was unyielding. The *Fitzgerald* began a long dive toward the center of the earth.

As the angle of her descent increased, the 26,000 tons of iron ore piled inside her began to shift, then roll, then topple forward. She started to accelerate. With the cargo falling forward, the air in the cargo hold rose toward the stern. At some point in the downward slide, the *Fitzgerald*'s after-end — funnel, poop deck, lifeboats, deckhouse, and propeller — lifted out of the writhing water.

As the free fall continued, the air inside was compressed against the roof of the long deck and the hatch covers, searching for weaknesses in the thousands of joinings that held the *Fitzgerald* together. Deep underwater, the running lights on the forward deckhouse continued to burn, tracing thin arcs of red, green, and yellow through the darkness. It was a slow-motion struggle between water, air, and steel.

It had taken more than a year to build the *Fitzgerald* into a steel ship an eighth of a mile in length. It took less than 10 minutes for the lake to break her apart. The destruction started at her midsection, the place of her beginnings, the locus of her greatest weakness. The sheet steel of her center — deck, bulkheads, and bilges — twisted and bent into grotesque geometries. Hull plates and deck plates ripped open. Hatch covers blew off. The deck crane separated from the main deck and tumbled into the blackness. As if in a dream, the bow section and stern section began to move in different directions.

Most of the suffering of steel took place in the black depths, beneath the howling winds, muted and murderous. Running through it were streams of air escaping through hundreds of openings. There were repeated concussions of impaled wood and glass. The ship dissolved with awesome rapidity. Unidentifiable pieces of steel separated from the hull, hung suspended for what seemed like an impossibly long time, and then arced forward along invisible trajectories. From somewhere out of the depths came a clear, distant sound, like a church bell ringing in the rain.

At one point, the lake invaded the engine room and strangled the generators and pumps. Throughout the ship, lights burned brilliantly, glowed red, and went out. For a brief time there was a fire inside the lake, burning brightly within the steel walls of the boilers, and then there was a pair of white magnesium flashes, a series of explosions, and the sound of crawling thunder. Under a writhing river of bubbles and chaotic eddies, the disintegrating ship and its disconnected fragments slammed into the vast sedimentary plains at the bottom of the lake. Her stern landed upside down. Her bow came to rest on its keel. On the surface, where the ship once had been, there was a wide area of black and white upwellings, and waves in every direction.

Chapter Seven

SILENCE IN THE WAVES

The searchers all say they'd have made Whitefish Bay if they'd put fifteen more miles behind 'er

Inside the pilothouse of the *Anderson*, the men stared ahead at a nightmare lake and the pale blur of a receding snow squall. The air inside the pilothouse smelled of wet wood and stale breath. With every wave, water pressed through invisible cracks in the windows and doors, creating a thin white fog on the glass of the compass. The compass card swung hard on its pivot, both ways, and then back toward the center. The wheel in the helmsman's hand, barely discernible in the dimness, had the appearance of a fragile wooden toy. No one spoke. The dominant sound was a clamorous patter on the windows and roof, mixed with howling winds that attacked the wheelhouse with sudden booming gusts.

"About 7:30 it cleared up. You could see for miles and we could see those three ships about 17 miles away coming up out of Whitefish Bay. The lights were clear. You could see their running lights. I turned to the mate and said 'Where's the Fitzgerald?' *We got out our binoculars and we started to scan the horizon. We thought maybe she had a blackout... Then we went to the radar and frantically tried to use its suppressor to bring us a target. We didn't get any. I got on the phone and called around the area. I called the saltwater vessels anchored behind Whitefish Point to see if they were getting any targets on radar. There just wasn't anything. She was just gone..."*

At first Captain Cooper and his men kept their reactions to themselves, fighting the reality of a wide reach of water that showed pinpricks of light in the distance, but nothing in between. They stared hard through the windows. One of them looked down continually at the yellow gleam rising from the radar screen. They saw nothing so they kept looking. For long seconds they kept the possibility of a doomed ship from entering their thoughts.

"We called the Coast Guard and tried to get some help. I talked to them briefly, but they were having their own problems at the Sault... all their communications were down. The wind had knocked out their antennas. They finally answered me. I had one hell of a time convincing them that the Fitzgerald *was gone. They kept reporting a 16-foot boat that was missing in Whitefish Bay. I said the* Fitzgerald's gone... *"*

It was 7:25 p.m. when Captain Cooper radioed the other ships in the area, asking if they could see the *Fitzgerald*. Another hour passed before he was able to contact the Coast Guard to report that he thought the *Fitzgerald* had disappeared. After his call, the watchstander on duty in Sault Ste. Marie tried to radio the *Fitzgerald*, but there was no response. At 8:40, Sault Ste. Marie informed the Rescue Coordination Center in Cleveland that there was uncertainty regarding the *Fitzgerald*. At 9:30, the *Anderson* called back, this time to confirm that the *Fitzgerald* was missing. Twenty-two minutes later, the Rescue Coordination Center directed the Coast Guard cutter *Naugatuck* to depart from Sault Ste. Marie, and the cutter *Woodrush* to depart from Duluth, some 300 miles to the west.

Inside the pilothouse of his ship, looking out on a remorseless lake, Captain Cooper was unable to fully comprehend what had happened. He stood there, swaying on his feet, the sweat of exertion upon his skin. There was no procedure, nothing in the regulations to prepare him for the sudden disappearance of a ship as big as the one he commanded. His thoughts raced out to the men who were on board the *Fitzgerald*.

The *Anderson* was kept on a heading that would bring her safely into Whitefish Bay. For all the men in the pilothouse, it was difficult to think clearly, so they held fast to their training. Each man scanned and re-scanned the horizon. And, without realizing it, each began the process of withdrawal and detachment to protect himself from thoughts that would later haunt him.

After a minor delay to put flares on board, the first Coast Guard aircraft, a fixed wing HU-16, took off from the Coast Guard air station in

Traverse City, Michigan, at 10:16 p.m. Seven minutes later, an HU-52 helicopter fitted with a 3.8 million candlepower xenon searchlight lifted off from the same airport. A second helicopter took off shortly after. A few minutes after midnight, all three aircraft were flying over the search area. Later they were joined by a C-130 Hercules from the Canadian Forces military base in Trenton, Ontario.

The lake was too hazardous for the Coast Guard cutter *Naugatuck*. This class of vessel was restricted from operating in winds greater than 60 knots in open water, and from proceeding beyond the entrance to White-fish Bay. She was further delayed by the failure of an oil-lubricating line, which kept her from arriving at the search area until 12:45 p.m. the next day. There were no other Coast Guard vessels of sufficient size to oper-ate safely in the existing weather conditions.

By about 8:45 p.m., Captain Cooper and his crew managed to bring the *Anderson* into the lee of Whitefish Point. The long spit of land to the west slowed the wild roll of their ship: imperceptibly, their deepest fears began to fade. Then, a little after 9:00 p.m., the commanding offi-cer of the Coast Guard at Sault Ste. Marie called and made a brief request. Would the *Anderson* reverse her course and assist the Coast Guard in its search?

> *"I am down in Whitefish Bay and I talk to Captain Miller, the best captain in the Sault, and he convinced me ... that we should turn around and go back. We had one really young gung-ho sailor ... he wanted to be in a storm ... when he found we had turned around he ran over and asked the chief engi-neer, 'Are we going back out?' When the chief said 'Yes,' the young sailor ran to his room, got his tape recorder and made out his last will and testament ... "*

By 10:30 p.m., the commanding officer of the Coast Guard had talked to the eight vessels anchored in or near Whitefish Point, asking them to join the *Anderson* in the search. He had also contacted three foreign-flag, oceangoing freighters, which were slightly northwest of the search area. Only one, the *William Clay Ford*, a Great Lakes ore carrier under the com-mand of Captain Don Erickson, responded positively. The officers on duty in the other 10 vessels said they were unable to proceed to the search area because weather conditions were too severe. It was an agonizing de-cision for a ship's captain to make. His first responsibility was for the safety of his ship and crew, but his heart opened to a sister ship in trouble.

The *Anderson* and the *Ford* arrived in the search area at about 2:00 a.m. The winds and the waves had diminished somewhat.

"...as we proceeded out there, I estimated the position of where the Fitzgerald disappeared, and went downwind. The wind was west-northwest...I stuck the nose of the ship right on a heading where the Fitzgerald would be ...and the debris should have been drifting. During this night search, when we were working with the Coast Guard, and with aircraft flying overhead, I said, 'Drop a flare on my deck so that I can see.' Flares are not what they are cracked up to be. With a big sea...It's hard to pick up a small object. When they drop a flare, it's kind of yellowish in the water. It doesn't give you good visibility. So they finally gave up dropping the flares."

It was pitch-black and the massive waves, with their steep sides and boiling edges, made searching for lifeboats and men in life jackets highly dangerous. Captain Cooper and Captain Don Erickson had never seen anything like it. Both ships held a gallant company of officers and men, all with pounding hearts, fully aware they might suffer the same fate as the *Fitzgerald*. It wasn't just the size and shape of the mountainous waves. It was their icy heart.

"We kept plowing around there trying to find survivors.... Those three salties [oceangoing freighters] were off their course a bit but they couldn't turn around. They said the seas were too big. They thought they'd turn over.... Thank God there were no other lake freighters in the area...they couldn't possibly have taken it. They would have just torn apart."

At 8:07 a.m. the next morning, the remains of the *Fitzgerald*'s number-one lifeboat was spotted approximately nine miles to the east. Its stern was sheared off. The port-side plating was buckled and pierced. The starboard grab rail was missing and the propeller shaft was distorted. The number-two lifeboat was sighted an hour later, about four miles south of the first.

During the next three days, a large number of items were recovered from the lake and along the Canadian shoreline. These included two rafts, twenty cork life preservers, or pieces of them, eight intact or broken oars, thirteen life rings, and one floodlight of the type mounted on

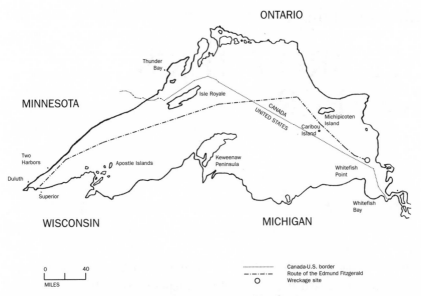

Lake Superior; showing the route of the Fitzgerald's *final voyage.*

Map: Lara MacInnis

the *Fitzgerald*'s pilothouse. Each was carefully lifted out of the water, photographed, and placed in a plastic bag.

For three days, several other large ships and additional aircraft joined in the search. Small parties of men in foul-weather gear walked slowly along the bays and coves of the Ontario shore. The storm blew itself out and was replaced by another one of less severity. On November 13, at 10:12 p.m., the official search was called off.

As her loss was reported to the Coast Guard, the *Fitzgerald* turned into a major news item, racing with the speed of light into and out of newsrooms and radio and television stations across North America. It had happened before with the loss of the nuclear submarine *Thresher* in 1963, and it would happen again with the sinking of the *Ocean Ranger* in 1982. There were no survivors and no bodies. Twenty-nine people were gone.

The families were as shattered as the ship. Company officials were stunned. Great Lakes ship captains shook their heads in disbelief. The Coast Guard began organizing an official inquiry. The 30 million people who lived next to the Great Lakes looked across their waters with renewed respect.

Chapter Eight

MY BROTHER'S KEEPER

The church bell chimed 'til it rang twenty-nine times
for each man on the Edmund Fitzgerald

It was still dark outside the rectory windows in Grosse Pointe Park when Father Richard Ingalls heard the telephone ring. Robert E. Lee's words came through the wire in short, clipped phrases. Curator of the Dossin Museum, Lee had spent most of the night listening to radio traffic coming down from the Soo. "The *Fitzgerald* is missing," he said. "They've been looking all night. They can't find her. Dammit, Richard, she's gone."

The two men were old friends and Father Ingalls knew that behind Bob Lee's salty demeanor was a heart ruled by compassion. Lee knew things that only men who have been out on the big lakes knew. Ingalls listened to his friend's words and understood what he had to do.

Father Ingalls was familiar with the tragedy of sudden death. For 10 years he had been the rector of Old Mariners' Church, attending to the blessings and travails of his parishioners. As a teenage sergeant first class in the Army Port and Service Command in the Second World War, he had suffered the loss of some of his closest friends. As a young married man he had experienced the shattering loss of his young son to sudden infant death syndrome.

Father Ingalls dressed quickly, shrugged on his dark blue overcoat, and went outside to his car. A soft gray light was beginning to rise out of the eastern rim of the sky. He carefully backed out of the driveway and a few minutes later was driving southwest along Jefferson Avenue toward Mariners' Church.

The small stone church, three blocks away from the Detroit waterfront, had first opened its doors in 1849. Modeled after similar churches built along the Atlantic coast, its mission was to minister to the hundreds of itinerant sailors who came into the harbor each week. In an evangelical and seafaring era, the church had been

Mariners' Church, Detroit, Michigan.
courtesy of Mariners' Church

dedicated to *"The Greater Glory of God, the only true and trusted pilot before whom we are all mariners combating the shoals of life."*

The rough sailors who manned the cargo ships with canvas sails felt very much at home inside the small stone church. There was something in the closeness of its black walnut pews, massive beams, and braces overhead that reminded them of their wooden-decked ship down at the harbor. With its silence and its sanctuary and its rich Rembrandt shadows, Mariners' was a refuge that enticed even the most ardent atheist.

The present church, with a cross at its peak and large Gothic windows, was built on land donated by Julia Anderson, a woman who had cared deeply about the men whose lives were spent far from the comforts of home. For more than 126 years its rectors and trustees held fast to the wishes of her generous bequest: Mariners' was to be an "independent church" open to all people "especially sea-going persons of whatever denomination."

As Father Ingalls steered his Oldsmobile down Jefferson Avenue, he thought of the hazards confronting sailors and the long history of ships being lost on the lakes. During the 10 years he had been rector, Father Ingalls had listened long and hard to the unburdening of souls and had thereby penetrated to a kind of truth. It was a truth about which Saint Paul had written, in which love, remembrance, and hope were joined.

Father Ingalls turned into the small parking lot on the south side of his church. Behind him, Randolph Street dived into the cavernous entrance of the mile-long tunnel to Canada. In the distance, a row of yellow lights winked on and off in the crosswaves of the river. The sky to the east was now several shades lighter than black.

Father Ingalls unlocked the large oak doors and walked past glass cases holding beautifully carved ship models, climbed a staircase, and entered the bell tower. The tower was cold; he kept his coat on as a shield against its chill.

The square stone tower was four stories high. Hanging from a steel beam just below its limestone battlements was the all-bronze three-thousand-pound Brotherhood Bell. Father Ingalls paused before its thick, white pull cord. He could see light just beginning to stream through a pair of tall stained-glass windows. At the peak of the east window was the outline of an old wooden ship with a cross-topped mast symbolizing the ship of the church. At the base of the window was a colorful rendering of a 20th-century ore carrier. Linking them together were the lead-framed words:

> *Thanks be to God for all seamen*
> *Who have given their lives in*
> *Service on the Great Lakes.*

Father Ingalls took a firm grip with both hands on the rope and began to pull. He didn't know the names of the captain and crew of the *Fitzgerald* but he knew there were 29 of them and so he rang the bell 29 times, pausing at the end of each long pull, feeling the sound coming down, hearing it ringing out through the louvers of the tower, ringing across Jefferson Avenue, and echoing off the curved glass buildings of the Renaissance Center. There was a steady rhythm to it now, a ringing and a pause and a ringing and a pause, the deep clear sound resonating through the cold half light of dawn, a rhythm that hinted of the alternation of life and death, the one springing up after the other, both arising when least expected. Finally, the melancholy voice of the bell became still and a cold silence crept into the tower.

The gray walls of Mariners' Church were penetrated by large stained-glass windows that splashed tropical colors across its interior. Looking down at Father Ingalls as he made his way to the altar at the sanctuary were Noah at the flood, Moses parting the waves, and pious figures of seagoing saints and apostles. Outlined in rainbow tracery beside them were the equally pious figures of a host of maritime explorers including Columbus, Raleigh, Drake, and Marquette.

Father Ingalls passed through the nave and the rails of the altar and went into the sanctuary, where he knelt at the prie-dieu. As he bowed his head, his thoughts went out to the *Fitzgerald*'s lost sailors. They were God's children. They were our brothers. Now that they are gone we cannot undo the event, but we can do something for them and that is to remember them. Remember them in the fullness of their lives. Remember them as men who were born, who laughed, who were loved, and who loved in return. That is all we can do and that is all they would ask.

A door opened and closed quietly at the far end of the nave. There was the muffled shuffling of feet followed by silence. Then it happened again. Father Ingalls kept his head bowed and continued his Devotions:

> *Almighty and everlasting God . . . Thank you for their courage and strength; for the benefits we have received from their labors and for the blessed hope of their everlasting life. We hereby gratefully remember them as we gratefully remember all the mariners of our Great Lakes who have lost their lives . . .*

The sounds were closer now, near the front of the church. Father Ingalls looked up and saw them. There were about 20 of them, perhaps 25, mostly men in neckties, some of them with their heads bowed, some with notepads and video cameras, and they were all looking directly at him. He waited for a moment then beckoned them closer. They stepped forward hesitantly, looked at their notepads, and began to ask questions. Had he heard about the *Edmund Fitzgerald*? Did the ringing of the church bell have anything to do with the loss of the ship?

One by one their questions were answered and they put away their notepads and video cameras and drifted out of the church, back to their newsrooms and editing suites, where they wrote their stories about a man who had none of the answers but whose private actions and words had expressed deeply felt emotions.

Their stories were picked up by the wire services and relayed across the country.

Chapter Nine

THE FAMILIES

And all that remains is the faces and the names
of the wives and the sons and the daughters

Early on the morning of November 11, 1975, John McCarthy was in Saint Croix in the U.S. Virgin Islands, getting ready to go to work. He turned on the radio to listen to the six o'clock news. The station manager, Bob Miller, whom he knew personally, reported on some international events. Then there was a short item about an iron ore freighter lost on the Great Lakes. The words lifted the hair off the back of John McCarthy's neck. John knew the lakes and he knew the ships. His father had been taking him on board the big freighters since he was 12 years old. At age 18, he spent the first of four summers working as a deckhand. Trying to collect his thoughts, he quickly dressed and drove over to Joe Lavin's house. "We heard it too," said his old friend.

McCarthy then called his mother in Cleveland and woke her from her sleep. "Mom, it's Johnny. What do you hear abut the *Fitz*?" There was a short silence and then a voice that seemed hollow and lost. "Johnny, it's terrible. They don't know where they are ..."

It was as if someone had stolen the oxygen from his lungs. There had been nothing in his fairly ordinary life—nothing in his years of schooling and hours of church-going—to prepare him for the enormity of what was happening. It took McCarthy two days to fly from Saint Croix to Cleveland, via Puerto Rico and Miami, and wherever he went, there was a radio, a newspaper, or a television station confirming that a big ship and her 29 men had disappeared in Lake Superior. His mind kept filling with memories. There were the summers on Lake Erie. There was the cold winter night when his mother bundled all four kids into the

car and drove to the docks in Toledo. His father, who had been away for
months, was coming in for a two-day layover. It was Christmas Eve and
the sky was filled with snowflakes, the kind that stick to a child's cheek.
They stood there for a while in the night hush, waiting, and then they
saw the glow of running lights behind the whiteness and then a bright
yellow light came on and there, on the ship's boom, was a fat man in a
red suit behind a team of reindeer with "Silent Night" playing on the
ship's loudspeaker.

His Uncle Jim, Jack's brother, met him at the airport with a big hug
and the words: "Many things in life are tough, Johnny. There have been
people coming to your house for two days and your mother has no idea
of what's going on. As the oldest in the family, you are going to have to
handle this..."

They left the airport, driving west and then north, and turned down
the street and into the driveway of the white-frame, red-brick house on
Webster Road. Big shade trees hung over the neighbor's fence. A
clipped lawn ran up from the street. The flower beds were empty, waiting for spring. Inside, a small group of people talked quietly and looked
at him with compassion. One by one, his mother, his brother, Dan, his
sisters, Beth and Mary Catherine, and Nelson Callahan, the pastor of his
church, held him in their arms.

Later, John McCarthy walked through the house, pausing in each
room — all reflected an aching emptiness. As he walked through the
kitchen, he stopped and looked out the window. He remembered a day
when he was in high school. Seventeen, cocky, and quick-tongued, he'd
just had another argument with his old man. He had been sitting alone
at the kitchen table when his father came in quietly and sat down across
from him. They both waited and then there was the soft Irish voice saying "You know, Johnny, we can't agree on anything, can we?" The son
hesitated before he answered. "You're right, Dad, we can't." A smile
flashed across his father's face. He reached across the table and touched
his son lightly on the forearm. "You see," he said, "we just did. Let's give
it a chance. Let's talk." And they did.

The thought of the inaccessibility of his dad's body added to the pain.
Jack McCarthy was lost under dark water, perhaps never to be found.
"How can we have a funeral?" was a question being asked by the
McCarthys and the other 28 families.

As the days passed, there was no peace, only a small anxious knot in the pit of the stomach that wouldn't go away.

⚓

On the evening of November 10, Janice Armagost turned her car onto the main highway leading east out of Superior, Wisconsin. The sky was black. The traffic was light in both directions. There were three other women in the car with her and they spent most of the 50-minute drive to Iron River discussing their children, their husbands, and what they had seen and done that day in downtown Superior.

The streets of Iron River were almost deserted. The sidewalks and lawns were covered with last night's snow. Three times, Janice stopped her car in front of a well-lit house and said goodbye to one of her friends. Then she was alone with the defroster's hum. Three miles outside of town, she gently braked the Ford and pulled into a gravel driveway beside a one-story ranch-style house. Before she had turned off the engine, the front door opened and an older woman appeared in the doorway. It was her husband's mother.

Janice closed the car door and walked quickly toward her.

"What's wrong?" she asked.

"Mike's boat is missing."

Janice caught her breath. "What do you mean Mike's boat is missing?"

"It's on television. Mike's boat is missing."

Janice ran through the open doorway into the living room and stopped in front of the flickering TV screen, which stood in the far end of the room.

It was not the words that frightened her, it was the look on the announcer's face. Jack McKenna was the weatherman for the station in Duluth and each night, after the evening news, he gave his description of the changing heavens with a combination of facts and breezy humor. Tonight, there was anguish in his eyes. He was standing in front of a large outline of Lake Superior. He turned and drew a circle around the area north and west of Sault Ste. Marie.

"This is where the ship was last heard from. This is where the storm was at its most ferocious..."

Janice looked around the living room. The green-flowered couch, the Ethan Allen end tables, everything was the same. But everything had changed. Suddenly, she realized that her body was shaking. She sat down on the couch and, for a moment, closed her eyes. Words kept coming out of the television set: "There is some hope that the *Fitzgerald* took shelter.... We'll bring you more information as soon as it comes in..."

She sat and listened and tried to take it all in, the enormity of what she was hearing. She thought about Mike and what they had had together and what might be no more. She stood and talked to Mike's mother, using words she no longer remembers. Later, she turned on the radio. She called her own mother in Madison, 300 miles away, who said, "I'll be right there." She called the Coast Guard in Superior, but as the hours dragged by, no one, not the Coast Guard, not the radio announcers nor the television anchormen knew anything for certain. At midnight, the television station went off the air and the small screen in the living room shimmered with blue snow.

She did not sleep. First thing in the morning, she was on the phone again, this time to the shipping company Oglebay Norton in Cleveland. A woman's voice answered and said she was sorry but she couldn't tell her anything because no one knew anything for certain. Janice waited for a while then called back and another woman's voice answered — or maybe it was the same one — and she asked, "What have you heard?"

"Nothing," Janice said.

There was a long pause on the other end of the telephone, as if the woman was taking a deep breath. "If you are going to have a memorial service, then I think you should go ahead with it."

And that was it from the big corporation that operated the multi-million-dollar ship, a few quiet words from within an office tower in Cleveland, a crisp summary of what Janice Armagost might do next. Oh yes, the company did send a wreath of white carnations to the memorial service, but as far as the executives of Oglebay Norton were concerned, there were other matters considerably more pressing than the grief of a woman in Iron River, Wisconsin.

Nothing pained Janice more than what she saw when she looked at the faces of her children. In less than a month, Chris would be three. Michele was almost six. What was she going to tell them?

She took Michele into their bedroom, closed the door, and looked down at the green eyes staring up at her.

"There's been an accident. A big storm. Daddy's boat sank." Janice took a deep breath. "Daddy won't be coming home. He's up in heaven with God."

They both started to cry.

"He won't be coming home again?"

"No."

"He's up in heaven with God?"

"Yes."

An hour later, she looked through the open door of the bathroom. Chris and his cousin Billy were standing in front of the sink, playing with a toy boat. The boat was red and had a single funnel. As she watched, Chris reached out and struck the boat with his tiny fist. Then he hit it again. His words were barely audible. "Daddy's boat down," he said.

Just before seven o'clock in the morning of November 11, Ruth Hudson was driving her 1974 Buick to her job at Bonnie Bell Cosmetics in Lakewood, a suburb west of Cleveland. The sky was hazy and overcast. She was driving east, along Center Ridge Road. At seven o'clock, the announcer listed items he would be reporting on after the commercial break. One of them was about a "giant ore carrier that had gone down in last night's storm in Lake Superior." Ruth Hudson kept on driving. She was certain that her son Bruce's ship was already in Detroit. The commercial, with its predictable words and music, seemed to last forever. Then: "The ore carrier was the *Edmund Fitzgerald*...there were no survivors..."

Ruth Hudson saw a parking lot coming up on the right-hand side of the road. She carefully braked the car and turned in. She stopped, left the engine running, turned down the volume of the radio, and listened to her racing heart. She waited for as long as she dared and then she was out on the road and heading in the opposite direction, back home, so she could tell her husband. She wanted to tell Oddis before he heard it from someone else. Oddis would know what to do. She drove quickly, looking for help from a policeman who usually directed traffic at one of the intersections. He wasn't there this morning and so she drove alone down Porter and across Lorain Road, through more than one red light, thinking it all must be a mistake, a terrible mistake.

She turned onto Butternut Ridge and then drove down Burns Road, with its straight black asphalt surface and grassy drainage ditches on each side, slim sidewalks set back from the road, and rows of single-story wood-frame houses with generous lawns. It was the same road on which Bruce used to ride his sleek, noisy motorcycle. Bruce always drove carefully, understanding the risks, keeping them under control.

And now his future was gone, lost inside the darkness of a big lake far to the north. She remembered driving him down to the docks a little more than a year before so he could join his first ship, the *Ashland*. She remembered how she fought back the tears until after they had said goodbye and watched him climb up the boarding ladder with his bags. As she was driving away, the man at the gate saw her tears and said quietly, "He'll be fine, ma'am. There are family men on these ships. They will take care of him."

She turned into the driveway at 5806 Burns, parked the Buick on the narrow concrete driveway next to the house, walked past the flower beds and up the center steps to the front door. Her hands were trembling. She had no idea how to break the news to Oddis.

She walked in and slowly closed the door behind her. He was standing in the hallway. Across the silence, they looked into each other's eyes. Ruth had been married so long to this sensitive man, she knew he was trying to read her face. Still, she stood there and said nothing. There were simply no words for this. Finally, as if gasping for air, she spoke the words about their only child. "The *Fitzgerald*'s gone down and there are no survivors."

Their silent grief was tangible. Ruth looked down the hallway toward Bruce's room and turned her head away. Then they both began to weep.

Later, Ruth called her sister, Betty, who lived a short distance away. Betty had heard the news and was going to call but couldn't bring herself to. Then, Ruth called someone that Bruce knew in the office at Oglebay Norton, but the man's sentences were full of pauses and words in between saying "...well we hope the antennae just blew away and they can't be reached right now and will call..." But then the news was on the radio again and on television and the phone kept ringing, over and over again, until there was no more uncertainty. There had been a terrible accident on the lake and no one knew why.

And so the news came at different times and different ways to the Kalmons, Beetchers, O'Briens, and all the other mothers and fathers and wives and children. There had been a storm and big waves and no distress call and no one knew anything for certain.

Each man on the *Fitzgerald* was a husband, a son, a father, or a brother. For those closest to them — wives, children, and parents — the news of the accident ushered them into a place they never wanted to be. Their old lives were wiped out, their futures clipped.

Early in the morning of November 14, a United States Navy Orion aircraft began a series of low altitude passes over Lake Superior, north of Whitefish Bay. Inside, a team of technicians studied long gray banks of electronic equipment used to detect submerged Russian nuclear submarines. For several hours, the four-engine aircraft flew a series of parallel tracks that would eventually cover an area of 100 square miles. At one point within the search area, the lights in a signal-processing unit began to pulse and grow bright. Before the flight, the men had calibrated their highly sensitive magnetic-detection equipment against a ship of the same size and with the same cargo as the *Fitzgerald*. Something in the water below was sending back data indicating a similar target. One of the men noted the location on a clipboard: 46° 59.9′ N., 85° 06.6′ W. The target was approximately 17 miles north of the entrance to Whitefish Bay.

On November 14, and for the next two days, the Coast Guard cutter *Woodrush* steamed slowly over the target area located by the Orion aircraft. Another storm was bruising the lake and it was difficult keeping the cutter on its heading at such a slow speed. Trailing over the stern of the *Woodrush* was a black wire leading down through several hundred feet of water to a small, silver, torpedo-shaped object. The E.G. and G.

model 250 side-scanning sonar, or "fish," as its operators called it, was emitting a constant stream of high-energy pulses that reflected off the lake bed, creating a continuous acoustic "photograph." Most of the images coming up through the cable showed a smooth, flat bottom, but at one point the smoothness rose suddenly into the shape of two large objects lying close to each other in 530 feet of water. Sonargrams do not reveal much detail, but each of the objects seemed to be about 300 feet long. The acoustically rough area between them was tentatively described as spilled cargo.

On Sunday, November 16, at 4:00 p.m., a memorial service for Bruce Hudson was held at the United Methodist Church in North Olmstead. The small brown church with the stained-glass windows was about a mile from Bruce's home. It was filled to capacity with a community of families and friends who were struggling to understand what had happened. There were so many descriptions in the newspapers and on the radio and television that it seemed as if there had been several different accidents. But one fact remained: the young man who had been an Eagle Scout, and a member of this congregation since he was 10 years old, was gone.

Because a child's death is unthinkable, it is the most painful grief to endure. For Ruth and Oddis Hudson, the very order of the universe had been altered. And so their families and friends, and Bruce's friends, and many people who didn't know them well but knew their pain, gathered around them that day. The Reverend Michael Williams and the Reverend Mark Collier led the service that celebrated Bruce's life.

"We have come to worship God and to celebrate before him the life of his servant, Bruce Hudson. Lord have mercy upon us."

They knelt together and they prayed together under the warm glow of the stained glass and they read the words from Psalms 30:4-5 ... *"Tears may linger at nightfall, but joy comes in the morning."*

Sitting quietly in rows, with upturned faces, the worshipers listened to the Memorial Meditation and then, with blended voices and bowed heads, they said the Lord's Prayer. Together they sang the concluding hymn, their voices hesitating on those parts that seemed especially poignant.

Michael Row the Boat Ashore ... The Jordan River is chilly and cold...
Kills the body but not the soul... The Jordan River is deep and wide ...
Milk and honey on the other side... Hallelujah.

Similar words in other hymns were sung in dozens of churches and chapels in Detroit, Michigan; Agoura, California; Duluth, Minnesota; Superior, Wisconsin; Fort Myers, Florida; West Lake, Ohio, and other towns and cities across the heartland of North America.

"O Lord, how do we know you? Where can we find you? You are as close to us as breathing and yet you are farther than the farthermost star. You are as mysterious as the darkness of the night and as familiar as the light of the sun.... We thank you, O God, that we have known your goodness in the life of your servant, Bruce. The beauty of his life remains with us as your living benediction. Praise to you, O God, the source of life. Amen."

At the end of the day, Ruth and Oddis Hudson—like the McCarthys, who lived only a few miles away—went home to an empty house with a small bedroom at the end of the hall. They would keep this room, with its two windows facing north and east, toward the lake, just as Bruce left it. His high-school trombone would lean against the wall. His Great Lakes charts would stay, rolled up. The books on advertising and botany would remain on the shelf. And the collection of color pictures, including the one of him as an Eagle Scout and the one of his dog, Kelly, would sit on the table facing the silent room.

Bruce's dark blue Kawasaki motorcycle would stay parked in the garage for almost 20 years. "You keep in your mind that he will come home," Ruth told me. In her heart, as in the hearts of all the others, there was confirmation that from the beginning of life to its end, love is the only thing that matters.

Chapter Ten

THE SONG

Gordon Lightfoot lives in a rambling red-brick Victorian house in downtown Toronto. It is handsome and high-ceilinged, with a wide front porch and a formal hall and staircase leading to its upper floors. On a snow-draped morning in January 1976, Lightfoot, wearing jeans and an old knitted sweater, walked up the curving staircase to the third floor, opened a door, and stepped into a small heated room. The room was fitted out like a captain's cabin with a white pine floor, a round table, and a wooden chair. Its single-framed window looked east through the trees toward a ravine and the Don River Valley. Lightfoot switched on the light, opened a black case, picked up his old Gibson guitar, and adjusted the chair. After he tuned the guitar, he began strumming a series of minor chords.

Lightfoot was 37 years old and at the peak of his creative career. For almost two decades he had traveled the long road from jazz drummer to barbershop-quartet singer to folksinger, from high schools to clubs to concert halls in hundreds of cities and towns in Canada and the United States. Lightfoot was a songwriter inspired by the land he lived in, the forests that seemed to run on forever, the divinely abundant waters that occupied the spaces between them and small northern towns like his hometown, Orillia, which struggled against freezing winters. At an early age, he discovered that Canada's big spaces contained a multitude of unvoiced narratives. Some were about blizzards and spring floods, others were about love and death. The best of them contained a mixture of both. By 1967, songs like "Early Morning Rain," "Sundown," and

"The Canadian Railroad Trilogy" had made him an internationally acclaimed writer and performer.

The small room with its sloped ceiling concentrated the sounds coming out of Lightfoot's guitar. He played a series of chords, changed them, played them again, wrote them down, changed them, and played them in that halting but effortless way an artist coaxes something new out of nothing. The chords were haunting and hypnotic.

Lightfoot spent the next three days isolated in the room working on the lyrics and music of the new song. He did not notice the light in the window slowly fading from gray to black. He ate sparingly. He was fueled by countless cups of coffee, glasses of whiskey, and the resolve to get it right.

The first thought that the story contained something important came to him on the night of November 10 during a newscast. The second came 10 days later after reading a two-column article in *Newsweek* magazine. Lightfoot had sailed the unforgiving waters of the Great Lakes and he sensed that the *Fitzgerald* story defied rational explanation. It had soul-honing grief. It had a lake that refused to give up its dead. Somewhere there were words and music he had been trying to capture all his life.

He had spent two months researching the story, reading all the newspaper articles his sister Beverly brought to him, thinking hard and making notes, trying to imagine the lake and the ship and the men and the chaos that joined them. Trying to imagine the lost families and the small church in Detroit where the bell had been rung 29 times. And for three nonstop days these thoughts and others poured in profusion from his brain to his muscular arms and deft fingers chording and strumming.

At the end of the third day, Lightfoot arrived at a combination of words and music that seemed right. He had compressed the story into a tone poem of eight verses and 430 words. He was relieved. It had been years since he had written a song of such personal importance in such a short time. He was working on a lot of other material for his new album. "The Wreck of the Edmund Fitzgerald" would be the album's final track. At 11:30 that night Lightfoot rose from the chair, put his Gibson back in its case, and left the room. As he closed the door and descended the stairs, he was holding a thin sheaf of papers.

It took Gordon Lightfoot and Terry Clements, Rick Haynes, and Peewee Charles two days and gallons of Irish coffee to record the song.

In less than a year, "The Wreck of the Edmund Fitzgerald" was one of the most popular songs in North America. As the years passed, the song and the shipwreck and the men and the lake became one.

The Wreck of the Edmund Fitzgerald

The legend lives on from the Chippewa on down of the big lake they called Gitche Gumee. The lake, it is said, never gives up her dead when the skies of November turn gloomy. With a load of iron ore twenty-six thousand tons more than the Edmund Fitzgerald weighed empty, that good ship and true was a bone to be chewed when the "Gales of November" came early

The ship was the pride of the American side coming back from some mill in Wisconsin. As the big freighters go it was bigger than most with a crew and good captain well seasoned, concluding some terms with a couple of steel firms when they left fully loaded for Cleveland

And later that night when the ship's bell rang, could it be the north wind they'd been feelin'? The wind in the wires made a tattletale sound and a wave broke over the railing. And ev'ry man knew as the captain did too 'twas the witch of November come stealin'

The dawn came late and the breakfast had to wait when the gale of November came slashin'. When afternoon came it was freezin' rain in the face of a hurricane west wind. When supper-time came the old cook came on deck sayin' "Fellas, it's too rough t' feed ya"

At seven P.M. a main hatch-way caved in; he said, "Fellas, it's bin good t'know ya!" The captain wired in he had water comin' in and the good ship and crew was in peril. And later that night when 'is lights went outta sight came the wreck of the Edmund Fitzgerald

Does anyone know where the love of God goes when the waves turn the minutes to hours? The searchers all say they'd have made Whitefish Bay if they'd put fifteen more miles behind 'er. They might have split up or they might have capsized; they may have broke deep and took water.

*And all that remains is the faces and the names of the wives and the sons
and the daughters*

*Lake Huron rolls, Superior sings in the rooms of her ice-water mansion.
Old Michigan steams like a young man's dreams; the islands and bays are
for sportsmen. And farther below Lake Ontario takes in what Lake Erie
can send her, and the iron boats go as the mariners all know with the
gales of November remembered*

*In a musty old hall in Detroit they prayed, in the "Maritime Sailors'
Cathedral." The church bell chimed 'til it rang twenty-nine times for
each man on the Edmund Fitzgerald. The legend lives on from the
Chippewa on down of the big lake they called "Gitche Gumee."
"Superior," they said, "never gives up her dead when the Gales of
November come early!"*

Chapter Eleven

THE OFFICIAL INQUIRY

Eight days after the accident, on the morning of November 18, a small group of men carrying heavy briefcases and wearing Coast Guard uniforms of senior rank walked through the glass doors of the Federal Building in downtown Cleveland and took an elevator to the thirty-first floor. When the elevator stopped and its door slid open, they stepped out, turned left, and made their way down the hallway to a small auditorium. At 10:00 a.m., the Marine Board of Investigation, with Rear Admiral Winifred W. Barrow as chairman, and Captains Adam S. Zabrinski and James A. Wilson as members, were sitting on one side of a long wooden table, looking out at the last people filing in and taking their seats. The auditorium was full. At 10:10, when the talking had stopped, Rear Admiral Barrow stood up and introduced himself. Barrow was the ideal admiral — tall, powerfully built, with black hair, a full, handsome face, and a deep theatrical voice.

"This investigation is intended to determine the cause of the casualty, to the extent possible, and the responsibility therefore.... The investigation and determinations to be made are for the purpose of taking appropriate measures for the promotion of safety of life and property at sea and are not intended to fix criminal and civil liabilities.

"The investigation will determine as closely as possible: One: The cause of the casualty; Two: Whether any failure of material, either physical or design, was involved or contributed to the casualty ... Three: Whether any act of misconduct, inattention to duty, negligence or willful violation of law on the part of any licensed or documented seaman

contributed to the casualty so that appropriate action may be taken...
Four: Whether any Coast Guard personnel or other representative
employee of the Government or any other person caused or contributed to
the cause of the casualty."

The auditorium was very quiet. A soft gray November light streamed
through the windows. Rear Admiral Barrow's voice was evenly modu-
lated, almost paternal. A livid, black lake and a big ship with solid tons of
water falling on her main deck and streaming out her scuppers seemed
far away.

It was the Marine Board's mandate to gather and record the facts of
the accident, either as part of a sworn statement or as hard physical evidence. In the coming days they would call in 45 experts in marine engineering, meteorology, seamanship, and ship handling, including former
captains, officers, and former crewmen of the *Fitzgerald*, and captains
and officers of other vessels. The focus of the board's questions was simple and direct. Was there a defect in the ship? Was there a flaw in the
loading or sailing procedures? Were the safety systems adequate? In all
the questions and in the tone of the testimony, there was an aura of iron
legality, as if the ship and her men were being tried in front of a jury.

There were, however, some serious constraints to the proceedings.
There were no survivors. The earnest men in the dark suits were con-
ducting a forensic audit of an event that no one had seen. And the bulk
of the evidence lay at the bottom of a deep lake. What remained of the
Edmund Fitzgerald belonged more to the watery darkness than the light.
Out of the twilight of such uncertainty, theories multiplied. One theory
was that the ship had suffered some kind of structural failure. Another
was that she had taken in water through an open hatch cover. Still
another was that she had bottomed out near Six Fathom Shoal.

The Marine Board officials sought to bring order to this disorderly
universe. One of the first individuals they called to the stand was Captain Bernie Cooper. Like many of the men who were out on the lake
that night, Cooper had a theory. As soon as he had docked the *Anderson*
at Sault Ste. Marie on the afternoon of November 11, he called the
Cleveland office of U.S. Steel and, in a recorded conversation with four
senior company officers, said: *"He went in close to the island and I am positive in my own mind — we had him on radar — I am positive he went over the
Six Fathom Bank... "*

One of the company's men said to Cooper "Bernie, I think we want you to say only what occurred as a matter of fact. "

"*I know*," said Cooper. "*You don't want to infer anything.*"

"I don't want you guessing as to what happened on their ship beyond the information that was directly related to you," the man told him.

The accident was being steered out of the realm of chaos, into the realm of rational thought. Give us the facts, the men in the navy blue uniforms said, only the facts. But, the turbulent ocean, the earth's atmosphere, and the human mind do not behave rationally. Irregularities in nature, and in human nature, have long been puzzles to law and science. As the people sitting in the auditorium were learning, the facts were there, but they were at once too many and too few, too contrary and too incomplete. The story of the accident, and thus of the ship and her men, was beginning to oscillate between fact and fiction.

After he listened to Captain Cooper's recorded telephone conversation, Rear Admiral Barrow questioned the captain about the *Fitzgerald's* position relative to Caribou Island and Six Fathom Shoal.

Barrow: "You have stated, 'He went in close to the island, I am positive in my own mind.... He went over that Six Fathom Bank...' That is a rather positive statement. Did you believe that to be true?"

Cooper: "I still believe that as far as the small scale chart was concerned. That is what I was using."

Barrow: "You believed at the time you made this that he went over Six Fathom Bank?"

Cooper: "Yes, I do."

Barrow: "And the third part of the transcript says, 'We were concerned that he was in too close, that he was going to hit that shoal off of Caribou.'"

Cooper: "The shoal water that extends out from Caribou, yes."

Barrow: "In earlier testimony before this investigation, you had concluded that the *Fitzgerald* was perhaps some four to five miles off Caribou. Would you care to comment on what appears to be a contradiction between those two positions?

For an instant, Cooper was inside his pilothouse, looking at a lake the color of lead, listening to the thunder on his roof, the minutes stretching into hours.

Cooper: "All we can do is give you what we hauled down as an impression. It was my impression … that he was closer than I wanted to be."

⚓

The days passed and the interrogation continued. By design, none of the questions brought anyone in the room too close to what *really* happened. The interior of the ship and the minds of her men were off limits to anything except the imagination. But there were a few in the auditorium who descended into the terror of a dying ship with the lake inside her, choking up every passage and quenching all her lights, stilling the wonderful elaboration of her machines, suffocating everything that breathed.

And the central question remained unanswered: Why did the *Fitzgerald* sink so quickly that no one had time to make a distress call?

At times the proceedings revealed glaring uncertainties. Captain Delmar Webster, who had served under McSorley on the *Fitzgerald*, testified that lifeboat drills were held every seven days. "He had boat drills once a week," Webster said. "It was noted in the log." Retired First Mate Gerald Lange, who had also served under McSorley, gave essentially the same answer: "We had weekly drills, and these drills were so noted in the pilothouse log." However, former *Fitzgerald* crewmen Hilson, Larson, Lindberg, and Garcia stated that when they worked under McSorley there had been no boat drills.

During some of the questions there were revelations about the confusion of daily life on board ship.

Zabrinski: "Mr. Hilsen, you indicated that the lifeboat station was the number one boat. Was that on the port or starboard side?"

Hilsen: "… I can't be specific. I always get that mixed up."

Zabrinski: "Mr. Hilsen, who are you kidding? Any boat you ever went on — how many boats did you say you were on?"

Hilsen: "About twenty-five."

Zabrinski: "Every ship you were on, boat number one was on one side and boat number two was on the other side, and don't try to kid me."

Hilsen: "I am not."

Zabrinski: "Don't tell me you were on twenty-five ships and you don't know where number one boat is. This is a serious matter here, and you have been evasive on every answer you have given.... Now, you answer. What side is the number one boat on?"

Hilsen: "Port side."

Zabrinski: "Are you sure of that?"

Hilsen: "No sir, I am not."

Zabrinski: "You're damn right you are not. You are not sure of anything..."

During a period of 12 days, the board of inquiry heard testimony from 45 witnesses and studied 361 exhibits, including photographs and artifacts. The record of the proceedings was transcribed into a document 3,000 pages in length. For a number of reasons, it would take almost two years before the board issued its final report. During the long interval, dozens of experts offered opinions on the cause of the accident.

Five months would pass before Superior would shrug off its shield of ice and permit the first close-up examination of the scene of the accident. In truth, the scene of the accident had been erased. The *Fitzgerald* had ended her life on the surface of the lake, turning into something that was no longer a ship. The men looking for facts could only look beneath the surface, at shards and sections of broken steel.

On May 20, 1976, the U.S. Coast Guard cutter *Woodrush*, with Captain Jimmie Hobaugh in command, moved into position over an unmarked spot on the lake. It was a clear spring day with waves running restlessly beneath the keel of his ship. At the three corners of a large and precisely positioned triangle, Hobaugh's men lowered a one-ton navy anchor attached to some 2,500 feet of six-inch nylon line and sections of heavy chain. It was backbreaking and perilous work made even more so by the winds rising out of the north. As the day drew to its close, two of the white anchor lines were drawn over the *Woodrush*'s fantail and one over her bow, where they were snubbed tight to winches. As night fell, the *Woodrush* was locked securely inside a three-point moor directly over the *Fitzgerald*.

As Captain Hobaugh recalled, "That night the wind gathered strength and came whistling out of the northwest at speeds up to 50 knots. The waves galloping past us were eight to ten feet high. Admiral Barrow and I stood in the bridge watching the weather deteriorate. After he went below I stayed up all night to keep an eye on things."

The storm lasted six hours. When it was over and the sun came up over the purple hills to the east, Captain Hobaugh looked out on a lake that had stolen two of his three bright orange marker buoys.

"The movement of the ship riding up and down on the mooring lines had pulled them deep enough to implode," he said. When the big spherical buoys were hauled back to the surface, they looked like they had been punched by a mountain.

"Then for the next seven days," said Hobaugh, "the lake just lay down and let us go to work. It was so calm it was eerie. I had 47 people on my ship and everyone of them spoke in their Sunday voices."

There were no sounds on the lake except the ship's generator and sailors hauling lines across the deck. The men on the *Woodrush* were grateful for the calm lake. It allowed them to lower their large underwater camera sled with an efficiency unknown in other waters.

On the deck of the *Woodrush* squatted a one-ton robot. Jammed inside its 15-foot pipe frame were four black-and-red ballast tubes for depth control, three propulsion motors, a 35-millimeter camera system, two black-and-white television cameras, mercury vapor lamps, a side-scan sonar, and a manipulator arm with a claw resembling a giant nut-cracker. Designed and built by the United States Navy, it was called CURV, for "cable controlled underwater research vehicle." All of its functions—positioning, observing, and recording—were controlled by men sitting at a console inside a nearby van.

CURV was the third in a series of remotely operated devices built by the U.S. Navy. In 1966, over Palomares, Spain, a U.S. Airforce B-52 collided with the aircraft that was refueling it. While the world held its breath, the first CURV was deployed into 2,000 feet of water to recover an H-bomb that had fallen into the ocean.

While Lake Superior lay quietly at its feet, CURV made 12 dives, logging a total of 56 hours of bottom time and recording 43,255 feet of videotape and 895 color photographs. At last the men in the dark blue suits had something physical to look at, something that told them something, even if it was only about the aftermath of the accident and not the accident itself. For hours the black-and-white images streamed up the long cable and into the control van. Typically there was water, an empty space except for countless tiny particles flashing white on the screen, and then, looming up behind them a bent slice of steel. As the camera came closer, the steel became a torn hatch cover. The bed of the lake below was soft and gray. When the robot's propulsion motors dipped too close, the silt blew up into pale curtains that obscured everything.

Then, as the robot lurched forward, there was more water, black corridors of it, filled with flat sediment, and occasional sections of fractured metal. For hours the robot flew across the lake bed. At one point, it ran into a wall of steel lined with welds and rivets. Higher up was a railing and then, behind that, the ship's name in black letters, the camera jerking and then still, the water clear and then cloudy. A door frame appeared, then a window, and another, and then the men in the control van were gazing into the pilothouse. Time stopped. Among the men, there was a strange calm, partly because they were witnessing the results of something no one could explain.

They kept the robot there for a long time, unable to pull it away from the section of the ship that revealed so much and so little. Bob Kutzleb, who was in charge of the underwater operations, explained, "We spent hours surveying the pilothouse and the area around it. We flew above it several times, trying new angles of approach, trying to look through the broken windows as best we could. It was damn hard work."

Even with the lake so calm, it was difficult maneuvering CURV with precision. The robot was heavy. Its surface cable dragged through the water. And always in the minds of the men working at the control console was the fear that if they brought CURV in too close, it would become entangled in the wreckage. Some of the men operating CURV called it "the dope on a rope."

But they bullied it and cursed it and it continued, in spite of its technical shortcomings, to collect haunting images of the reshaped *Fitzgerald*. Nothing moved the heart to wonder more than the discovery of a huge hill of steel, a slope that seemed to rise forever under the ghostly wash of the lights, no portholes or wire railing, just a curving slant of steel painted a pale color, and then the camera showed them the bronze propeller suspended like a giant open flower. They stared at the propeller, trying to orient themselves to its startling position. Common sense told them that it should be buried deep in the sediments. Suddenly the realization hit them that, when the ship broke in two, her stern had rolled over until her keel and bottom plates were pointing at the sky. And in all the eyes gazing at the television screen there was a sorrow for what was already beyond their imagining.

On April 15, 1977, the Coast Guard issued its final report. The thick, bound volume represented months of study; an exhaustive review of all the still photographs and videotapes and thousands of pages of testimony from men who had served on her before the accident, or who had loaded her cargo the day before, or who were on other ships the night she went down. There was also testimony from men who worked for the Coast Guard, the American Bureau of Shipping, and the National Weather Service. Among its conclusions were:

- There is no evidence of actionable misconduct, inattention to duty, negligence, or willful violation of law or regulation....
- The nature of Great Lakes shipping with short voyages much of the time in very protective waters...leads to complacency and an overly optimistic attitude concerning...extreme weather...
- The loading manual which was developed for the *Fitzgerald* did not comply with the requirements of the load line regulations. Since the only loading information available...is the total cargo carried on downbound voyages...whether the *Fitzgerald* was ever subjected to unacceptable stresses cannot be determined.
- The system of hatch coamings, gaskets, covers and clamps installed on *Fitzgerald* required continuing maintenance and repair, both from routine wear because of the frequent removal and replacement of the covers and from damage which regularly occurred during cargo transfer...the system...did not provide an effective means of preventing the penetration of water into the ship...
- Whether all the cargo hatch clamps were properly fastened cannot be determined.
- The cargo hold was not fitted with transverse water-tight bulkheads. As a result...flooding water...could migrate throughout the hold.
- The position of *Fitzgerald* relative to that of *Anderson* cannot be reconstructed. Information available is based on the recollection of the

master and watch officers on *Anderson* ... testimony on these observations is inconsistent.

- *Fitzgerald* reported the loss of two vents and some fence rail, indicating that topside damage had occurred to the vessel. The flooding which could be expected to result from the loss of any two tank or tunnel vents would not be serious enough, by itself, to cause the loss of the vessel.

- *Fitzgerald* reported that steps were being taken to deal with the flooding and the list, and that two pumps were being used. *Fitzgerald* had four 7,000 GPM pumps and two 2,000 GPM pumps available, indicating that the flooding was evaluated ... as not sufficiently serious to create a danger of loss of the vessel.

- The cargo hold was not fitted with a system ... to detect water. ... It is concluded that the flooding of the cargo hold was not detected.

- Topside damage could have been caused by the vessel striking a floating object ... this could have resulted in undetected damage ... above or below the waterline ... the most likely area would have been in the forward part of the ship.

- Topside damage could have been caused by some unidentified object on board breaking away in the heavy seas. ... The only items on deck which had enough mass to do sufficient damage ... were a hatch cover, the hatch cover crane or the spare propeller blade.

- The topside damage and list could have been caused by a light grounding or near grounding on the shoals north of Caribou Island. Although the testimony is not fully consistent, both the master and watch officer on *Anderson* indicated that *Fitzgerald* passed within a few miles of Caribou Island. ... The vessel could have been damaged from the grounding, from the effects of the violent sea which would be expected near the shoals, or from the shuddering that the vessel would have experienced as it passed near the shoals. The damage could have been on deck, below the waterline or both ...

- The list could have been caused by a localized hull structural failure, resulting in the flooding of a ballast tank or tanks. ... The survey of those parts of the wreckage which could be seen showed no evidence of brittle fracture.

- The winter load line ... allowed 3 feet 3¼ inches less minimum freeboard than had been allowed when the vessel was built in 1958 ... the reduction in minimum-required freeboard significantly reduced the vessel's buoyancy ... it resulted in ... increased frequency and force of boarding seas.

- In the absence of more definite information ... and in the absence of any survivors or witnesses, the proximate cause of the loss ... cannot be determined.

The Marine Board of Investigation had given credence to the theories that everyone had been talking about for almost two years. But the men in the navy blue suits knew they had to do better than this. They had to come up with an answer that was more specific, an event that initiated the flooding. So they took a deep collective breath and pointed their fingers at the hatch covers:

> *Throughout November 10th the vessel was subjected to deteriorating weather and an increasing quantity of water on deck. With each wave that came aboard, water found its way into the cargo hold through the hatches. As the vessel lost freeboard because of this flooding and as the sea conditions worsened, the frequency and force of the boarding seas increased, and so did the flooding. The Master of the vessel reported that he was in one of the worst seas he had ever seen. It is possible that, at the time he reported this, Fitzgerald had lost so much freeboard from the flooding of the cargo hold that the effect of the sea was much greater than he would have ordinarily experienced. Finally, as the storm reached its peak intensity, so much freeboard was lost the vessel was unable to recover. Within a matter of seconds, the cargo rushed forward, the bow plowed into the bottom of the lake, and the midship's structure disintegrated, allowing the submerged stern section, now emptied of cargo, to roll over and override the other structure, finally coming to rest upside-down atop the disintegrated middle portion of the ship.*

And in case anyone missed it, they repeated it:

> *The most probable cause of the sinking of the S.S. Edmund Fitzgerald was the loss of buoyancy and stability which resulted from massive flooding of the cargo hold. The flooding of the cargo hold took place through ineffective hatch closures ...*

And with these words written by Rear Admiral Barrow, Captains Zabrinski and Wilson, and Commander C.S. Loosemoore the debate began. Within weeks, the Lake Carriers Association, which represented 15 domestic shipping companies with 135 vessels, was working on the draft of a letter to the National Transportation Safety Board. The first sentence of the letter stated that the association "completely rejects the Coast Guard theoretical cause of the *Fitzgerald* sinking." For the next 20 years, this difference of opinion would dominate all discussions about the *Fitzgerald*.

PART TWO
THE DIVES

Chapter Twelve

THE FIRST DIVES

Lake Superior, July 1994

The night before, the rain had fallen unceasingly. For several hours the black surface of the lake lay almost motionless beneath the downpour, but at long intervals it raised itself up and broke against the shore.

By mid-afternoon, the sun had driven all the clouds from the sky. The lake appeared vast and unconquerable. Then, without warning, a line of small bubbles appeared on its surface.

In the deep green water below, a flash of silver and yellow appeared, small and rising. As it continued its ascent, the yellow object enlarged and became rectangular. Finally, as it reached the sunlit depths, it revealed the shape of steel and fiberglass with a dome of clear plastic fixed to its front. The water around it filled with the sounds of humming. Bubbles scattered in every direction. Then, the research sub broke through the surface of the lake.

Clelia was the best of the current breed of shallow-water submarines. Slightly larger than an extended minivan, her design was inspired by the immutable fact that the human body needs protection from the cold and extreme pressure of deep water. Her most distinctive feature was a see-through bow that gave her three occupants a panoramic view of the inside of the lake. Fastened to brackets around this big window were scientific sampling devices, a television camera, and a pair of high-intensity lights. For the next few minutes, *Clelia* lay on the surface, rolling slightly, her yellow conning tower projecting above a wreath of bubbles.

About 200 yards away from the sub's bow, a white ship approached cautiously. Along both sides of her hull, large black letters spelled out the name of her owner: Harbor Branch Oceanographic. Until six years ago, the ship had been used to transport men and equipment out to the oil rigs in the Gulf of Mexico. At her new home port in Fort Pierce, Florida, she was converted into a comfortable, long-deck research ship, 168 feet in length. Across her stern was painted the name of the acclaimed aviation and undersea pioneer who had cofounded Harbor Branch, *Edwin A. Link*.

Clelia had just completed the fourth in a series of dives to the *Edmund Fitzgerald*. The air next to her filled with the whirring of thrusters and the sound of men talking to each other over submerged intercoms. She held her position, waiting for the *Edwin Link* to glide in close enough for a swimmer in a wet suit to jump into the water and hook a white nylon line to her bow.

Fourteen years ago, the crew of Jacques Cousteau's *Calypso* recovered their two-man sub from this same spot. As part of a natural-history film on the Great Lakes and Saint Lawrence River, Albert Falco and Colin Meunier made a single 30-minute dive to the *Fitzgerald*'s bow section. What they saw led them to believe that the ship had broken in two on the surface. Nine years later, an expedition organized by Michigan Sea Grant lowered a remotely operated television camera from the research vessel *Grayling* and shot five hours of color videotape. Among the expedition's findings were tons of taconite cargo spilled across the top of the forward section. The port-side pilothouse door was open. The experts who studied the videotapes concluded that they did not contain enough information to determine the cause of the sinking.

The *Fitzgerald* mystery continued to feed on uncertainty. Much of the fuel came from the letter written by the Lake Carriers Association to the National Transportation Safety Board 18 years earlier. The letter was signed by Paul E. Trimble, a former vice admiral of the United States Coast Guard. Trimble had two objectives. First, he wanted to convince the board and the Coast Guard that water did not enter the *Fitzgerald* through her hatch covers. Second, he wanted them to believe that she had been mortally damaged sailing over Caribou Shoals. He wrote:

> *There was no report of hatch damage or hatches opening up. Water on the main deck would have resulted in compressive action, pushing the hatch covers more tightly on their gaskets, rather than lifting them....*

The present hatch covers are an advanced design...the one piece covers have proven completely satisfactory in all-weather operations without a single vessel loss in almost 40 years of use...

The inspection...conducted ten days before the sinking by the Coast Guard...and the American Bureau of Shipping...revealed no significant damage of the hatch coamings or closure fittings.

The hatch covers (as seen on the 1976 video) could have been blown off by the compressed air in the cargo compartments as water entered from the sides or the bottom. This is a well known phenomenon based on experience in vessel sinkings. Or the hatch covers could have sprung from the weight of pellets as the vessel dove to the bottom.

...On page 2149 of the Board report Captain Cooper stated that he simultaneously had both the Fitzgerald *and* Caribou *(Island) on his radar and he was positive the* Fitzgerald *went over the shoals...*

The result of the hydrographic survey of the Caribou Island shoal waters ...identifies a shoal less that six fathoms deep more than one mile farther east than any...depicted on the latest navigational charts.

...Minutes after passing Six Fathom Shoal Fitzgerald *reported a list, two ballast tank vents carried away and that two ballast pumps were in use. Capacity of the two pumps were 14,000 gallons per minute...the amount of water entering two eight inch vents could readily have been handled by the two ballast pumps...Within the time frame involved, such a list can only be explained by holing of the vessel's ballast tanks caused by striking Six Fathom Shoals...*

...The lake shipping industry and its professional naval architect advisors can find nothing...to support the Coast Guard thesis that the sinking resulted from poor hatch closure procedures...(other) factors...support shoaling as the cause of the sinking.

Everyone who studied the *Fitzgerald* came away with an abiding uncertainty. A shipwreck is not like an aircraft accident. There is no black box to capture voice recordings and other vital data. And, given the size and location of a shipwreck, it is impossible to pick up the pieces and reassemble them in an attempt to understand the forces that sent them flying apart.

After the thick nylon line was hooked into the nose of the sub, the *Link* steamed slowly through the water, coming abreast, and then passing, the smaller craft. The tow line lost its slack just as a wave of energy pulsed down the line from the mother ship and urged her forward.

As the *Link* continued forward, *Clelia* glided around into the protective lee of the ship's stern. A big, deck-mounted winch tugged gently on the tow line until the transparent nose of the sub was a few yards behind the *Link*'s transom. *Clelia* was now under the arch of a giant steel A-frame that would pick her up and place her on deck. The wet-suited swimmer standing next to *Clelia*'s conning tower reached up and pulled down a stainless-steel locking pin attached to the main lift line. Caught by a whorl of hidden turbulence, the sub drifted to the right of the big ship's wake and then returned to its center. The swimmer, a young man in his twenties, waited and then pressed the heavy stainless-steel locking pin into its female socket. There was a deep clicking sound. When the swimmer stood up, he was smiling like a Masai warrior.

At this point, the water holding the sub began to vibrate with the power of metal under tension. From inside the ship came the sound of electrical generators and hydraulic pumps lifting *Clelia* free of the lake's grip. Water drained from her belly and then she was in the air, in the midst of an arc. Men tugged at lines. Engines roared. As she landed in her cradle, *Clelia* lost her awkwardness and became an integral part of the ship. Men ducked under her belly and secured tie-down cables. A

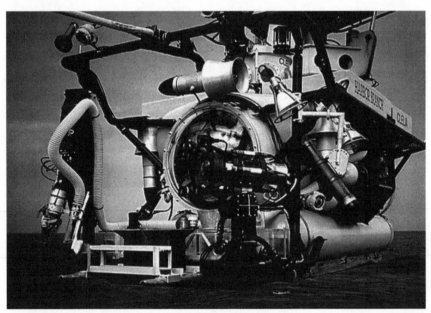

Launching Clelia *from the stern of the* Edwin A. Link.

Photo: Dr. Joseph MacInnis

ladder was placed against her starboard side. Before he opened the round metal hatch on top of the conning tower, the swimmer wiped off the last drops of water.

The defining word in the minds of all the men working on *Clelia* was *safety*. There wasn't a sub pilot or electronic technician on board who didn't know the details of a hot June day 21 years earlier when a similar sub operated by Harbor Branch became trapped on the sea floor. The accident happened northeast of Key West on the edge of the Gulf Stream. During a routine dive into 350 feet of water to collect biological samples, the sub became entangled in a slim, black wire attached to a scuttled U.S. Navy cruiser. As each rescue attempt failed, the oxygen supply inside the sub dropped, the carbon dioxide level climbed to toxic levels, and the hull turned ice-cold. When the sub was recovered at noon the next day, the two men in the aft chamber were not among the survivors.

Every routine, every checklist, every piece of safety equipment on the deck of the *Edwin Link* had been designed with this event in mind. Self-rescue—not having to wait until someone else comes to assist you, and then finding out they can't solve your problem—was a commitment running through the mind of everyone on board. At the center of this self-rescue ethic was a six-foot-high vehicle with video eyes, hydraulic muscles, and a wrist-thick lift cable that squatted on the deck a few steps away from *Clelia*. Painted the same lemon yellow as the sub, the remotely operated rescue vehicle was commanded by an engineer working at a console inside a control van. The vehicle had been used to survey the *Fitzgerald* before *Clelia*'s first dives. Its video did not reveal any entanglement hazards. In the event of an emergency, it could be launched and working at the *Fitzgerald*'s depth in less than 10 minutes.

The first person to climb up through *Clelia*'s conning tower was a young woman wearing a blue jumpsuit and a big smile. Anne Swardson was an internationally acclaimed journalist who wrote for the *Washington Post*. It was her first dive in a research sub. This is what she told me.

"Everybody has heard of the song, but the average American knows only that a ship called the *Edmund Fitzgerald* went down in the Great Lakes. I wanted to tell the story of the accident and this expedition to a wider audience.... All through the dive I kept asking myself, 'What are the words for this?'

"As we descended through the water, the colors changed from a near blue to green to dark green to black. When we turned on the lights near the bottom, the lake came alive. The bottom looked like beach sand.

"As we went along, we saw piles of taconite pellets...then a piece of jagged metal...then another. Then we saw the starboard side of the bow. It was so high I had to lean back...

"On the starboard side of the bow we saw two deep gashes. One ran through the M and the U in *Edmund*. The other ran through the L and the D in *Fitzgerald*. They were symbolic of the destruction of both the ship and its name...

"What struck me most was the absolute stillness of everything — there was a blanket and a sweater hanging partway out of a porthole — and the power of the forces that caused them to be there...

The pilothouse of the Fitzgerald.   Photo: Harbor Branch Oceanographic

"What I saw reminded me of a story I once read about the aftermath of nuclear war. A house was still standing, but all that remained of the people were shadows imprinted on the wall...."

The second person to climb out of the research sub was Tim Askew, Sr. During his 18 years with Harbor Branch, Askew had logged more than 900 dives. In his thousands of hours underwater, he had seen everything from rusting drum barrels containing nuclear waste to the broken hull of *USS Monitor*, the U.S. Navy ironclad whose duel with *CSS Virginia* in 1862 marked the birth of armor-plated ships. Askew had risen through the ranks to become Harbor Branch's Director of Marine Operations. When he spoke, recalling his impressions, he spoke slowly.

"Seeing the *Fitzgerald* from inside the sub is much more effective than seeing it through the television camera of a remotely operated vehicle. The sub's big dome window let us see things in full color and three dimensions…

"We first touched down in a big field of taconite pellets and clay. There were mounds of taconite everywhere. Our sonar showed us where the bow was and we tracked north toward it. All around us pieces of the ship stuck out of the mud like headstones… We were just above the lake bed when we saw the bow. It filled the window. There was nothing but steel going straight up. Black steel and the ship's name in white letters…"

At this point, Askew stopped talking and glanced across the lake. Last week he was at a shipyard that over a period of two months had taken his biggest research ship, cut it in two, inserted a 30-foot section, and welded everything back together again. I think he was comparing the energy required to do this with what he had just seen underwater.

Askew continued his account: "The stem [point of the bow] is the strongest part of the ship. But the *Fitzgerald*'s lower stem is bent at a right angle toward the starboard side. When the bow smashed into the bottom, it dug in deeply and plowed forward. There is a mound of silt in front of the bow that must be 15 feet high… The forces of impact were so fierce that they ripped the bow apart. There is a wide gash that runs through the name on one side down under the hull and up through the name on the other side.

"We flew past the pilothouse toward the stern and descended. The port side of the vessel is buried up to her main deck. We were moving aft looking at the upper hull plates when suddenly we saw the ribs near the bottom. Everything—plating, beams—was upside down and twisted into bizarre shapes. I think this happened as the after-end of the ship was torqued off the forward end…

"We flew back to the pilothouse, touched down on the waist-high railing, and looked in through the open windows. The port door was undogged and open… There was a pile of debris—it was impossible to tell what was inside it—on top of and below the chart table.... Next to one of the forward windows a black phone was hanging on its cable.

"All of us who work at sea are brothers in the trade. I felt like I knew those men. They've been on every ship I've ever served on. I wanted to stay there looking in, trying to understand what happened. But I didn't want to stay too long."

Six dives were made in *Clelia* to the bow and stern sections and the scattered metal pieces between. Two video cameras recorded the highlights. The track line of each dive was carefully noted and the pilots and observers debriefed as soon as the sub was safely on deck. Under the direction of Peter Scheifele, a marine science educator from Connecticut, and five Canadian and American high-school students working on the *Edwin Link*, a detailed site map of the wreckage was constructed. Its long list of observations include the following:

- The angle of the bow section and the position of the articles seen inside it indicate that the impact with the bottom projected everything to the port side.
- Inside the pilothouse the engine order telegraph, radar stand, water fountain and ship's wheel were intact. The engine order telegraph was set in the "all ahead full" position.
- The port pilothouse door was open; its locking dogs were undamaged and set in the open position.
- On the pilothouse roof the ship's brass bell was in place and undamaged. Its clapper and lanyard were still attached.

As soon as the last dive was completed, the *Edwin Link* headed south toward Whitefish Bay, following the course that the *Fitzgerald* never completed. The sky was overcast; the air was cold. As we read our notes and looked at the video, we came to understand the contours of the mystery. We might learn something about *how* the *Fitzgerald* sank, but we would never know *why* it sank. The *why* had been blown apart when 40,000 tons of runaway steel collided with the earth. We had a picture, but we didn't have an explanation.

Chapter Thirteen

FOR SALE: THE SOUL OF A SHIP

On a warm morning in May 1995, the wooden door of a small court-room in Lansing, Michigan, opened and the Honorable Lawrence M. Glazer took his position at the bench. Tall and distinguished, Judge Glazer looked down at his windowless courtroom like a headmaster at the beginning of the school year. Judge Glazer's court held about 25 spectators, some in navy blue uniforms with gold-braided sleeves, sitting on chairs behind a low, wooden railing. Seated at small tables in front of the railing were the plaintiff, Fred Shannon, and the defendant, Tom Farnquist. Shannon and Farnquist were short, dark-haired men in their late thirties. Neither man smiled.

Both men were products of the great American free-enterprise machine that slices and dices violence and tragedy into books, movies, talk shows, and whatever else might make a buck. Both men were ob-sessed with the *Edmund Fitzgerald*. They knew every detail of the voy-age, the sinking, and the search. For years they had been working on ways to cash in on the emotional appeal of the story.

In the 1970s, Farnquist was an amateur scuba diver living in Sault Ste. Marie, Michigan, who became fascinated with the shipwrecks lying at the bottom of Whitefish Bay. In 1978, he and some fellow divers founded the Great Lakes Historical Shipwreck Society. As the years passed, Farnquist built a small museum at Whitefish Point and acquired a reputation for being "ethically challenged." He also acquired a roomful of nautical objects lifted illegally from the lakes.

Fred Shannon was also a scuba diver. A former policeman and private investigator, he was now the owner and general manager of Metro-Media Entertainment, a one-man business that he ran from his home in Flint, Michigan. Like Farnquist, he became fascinated and then consumed by the story of the *Edmund Fitzgerald*. Both men recognized that the tragedy had all the ingredients to grab people's attention. A big ship that wasn't supposed to sink. The sudden and mysterious death of 29 men. They also knew that whoever could unravel the mystery of why she sank—or claimed to have the answer—would achieve considerable notoriety. And there were the commercial possibilities. It was the kind of story that could generate a best-selling book, fee-paying lectures, and a network television special.

A few years earlier, the two men had been friends linked by their enchantment with the same shipwreck. Then they had a debate about the use of an underwater videotape for a lecture. The debate became a simmering dispute. Jealousy and self-righteousness took over and they began to rage at each other in private and in public, calling each other names, shredding each other's reputations. Their rivalry was all the stronger because it was based on absolutely nothing. Having every reason to be nice to each other, their hatred was all the fiercer.

A year before, their struggle to exploit the *Edmund Fitzgerald* for self-promotion and financial gain turned into a race to see who would be the first to dive and survey the *Fitzgerald*. Using his museum's money, Farnquist paid ten thousand dollars to join the three-day Harbor Branch Oceanographic expedition. He and two of his associates each made a dive and took still pictures. A few weeks later, Shannon upped the ante and shelled out $75,000 of his own money to hire a ship and a stern-launched sub. He and his team made eight dives and shot 10 hours of videotape. That day, in court, the combat had shifted away from the lake and into a new theater. Shannon had filed a lawsuit to block Farnquist's plan to remove the ship's bell.

Tom Farnquist had been dreaming about the bell on top of the *Fitzgerald*'s pilothouse roof ever since he first saw it with an underwater video camera six years earlier. If he could organize an expedition to recover it, the effort would generate widespread publicity for his museum and a host of new products—posters, sweatshirts, home videos, coffee mugs—for his retail gift shop. Sales would be so brisk he might

have to build a new gift shop. The bell would be the gleaming center-
piece of a new museum building. His name would be on national television and in local newspapers. There was only one problem. Although
the *Fitzgerald* was an American ship, it lay in Canadian waters under the
jurisdiction of the province of Ontario.

Farnquist knew that the province, and its underwater archeologist,
did not look kindly on the removal of historical artifacts from its shipwrecks. He also knew that legitimate credentials and substantial effort
were needed to obtain an archeological licence. His record of illegally
removing artifacts from the state of Michigan waters might diminish his
chances. To succeed, he needed some velvet leverage.

To everyone's surprise, it was his arch-rival Shannon who unwittingly
gave it to him. During Shannon's July expedition to the *Fitzgerald*, a
man's body was sighted near the port side of the pilothouse, not far from
the open door. The frozen figure was fully clothed, wearing an orange
life jacket and lying facedown in the sediment. Shannon filmed the body
and then described publicly what had been found. His repeated descriptions created a minor media frenzy. Then he went on to claim that "the
body's location, attached life vest and other information...is helping to
piece together the cause of the tragic event." He was writing a book. He
was giving lectures, and had a television special in the works. But Shannon had gone too far. The families were furious. The sacred remains
might have been their husband or their son and Shannon was behaving
as if he owned those remains. The families agreed that something had to
be done.

Farnquist sensed an opportunity. He befriended two family members,
both women, one who had lost a son and another who had lost a father.
He assured them that he shared their view of Shannon's behavior. He
told them that he would be happy to assist them in preventing him from
diving again at the site. The two women liked the short man with the
serious face who listened so attentively and agreed so readily. After 19
years, it was comforting that someone was so interested in what they had
to say.

As time passed, Farnquist introduced his idea of making one last
dive to recover the bell. He suggested that the bell be placed in his
museum "as a memorial to the lost crewman." After the bell was recovered, he told them, the *Fitzgerald* would be placed "off limits to divers."

Farnquist asked if the women would help him in a letter-writing campaign to convince the other *Fitzgerald* families. He knew that with enough support it might be possible to pressure the Ontario government into granting a licence to recover the bell "on humanitarian grounds."

It worked. Writing from a text prepared by Farnquist, the women, joined by a third, sent out form letters to as many family members as they could find. Most of the handwritten responses were in favor of the project. "It would be nice for the men to be remembered," said some. "It would be a fitting memorial," wrote others. As if sensing the oncoming controversy, one young woman wrote: "I believe the only place the bell belongs is with the ship. A memorial at Whitefish Point is very important, but could be done just as tastefully without the bell. To retrieve the bell would be like desecrating the site." Farnquist photocopied the letters and sent them to the Ontario government. The official response was expected in a few days. Indications were that a licence would be granted.

In all his conversations and correspondence with the *Fitzgerald* families, Farnquist never mentioned how much money his not-for-profit museum was already making from the "selling" of the *Edmund Fitzgerald*. And how much the revenues were expected to increase when he added the ship's bell to his list of attractions. A high-profile diving expedition leading to the recovery of the bell could generate hundreds of thousands of dollars in general admissions, museum-theater revenues, home videos, and retail gift sales. And in all the conversations and correspondence, there was no offer to share any of these revenues with the families.

In recent months Shannon had watched Farnquist's activities with increasing concern. If Farnquist got permission to recover the bell, it would severely restrict Shannon's ability to cash in on his own expedition. To stop him, Shannon now had to convince a stern-looking judge.

What frustrated him more than anything on this fine spring day was what he *couldn't* tell the judge and the people in the courtroom. That Farnquist had a long history of illegally removing archeologically significant objects from shipwrecks. That the state of Michigan had filed a civil-action suit against him. That the Department of Natural Resources had issued a search warrant to enter his museum and seize its contents.

That after months of legal maneuvering, Farnquist had been forced to publicly apologize for his behavior and agree to comply with the law. In addition, there was Farnquist's two-year violation of the copyright law on Gordon Lightfoot's song.

Like everyone else who had taken an opponent to court, Fred Shannon was discovering that he had to play by the court's rules. He had to stay focused on the proceedings. His major legal tactic was to get his lawyer, Michael Rizik, to convince the tall judge with the bushy eyebrows that the wreck site was under American, not Canadian, jurisdiction. After glancing at this notes, Rizik spoke directly to the bench.

"Official government documents, specifically Coast Guard documents, Coast Guard maps, an engineering study that was done based on the co-ordinates Mr. Shannon collected...give us good reason to believe that at least a major part, or a part of the *Edmund Fitzgerald*, lies in Michigan waters."

More than one mouth dropped open at this information. In 20 years of studies, analysis, and reports, no one had ever suggested that the *Fitzgerald* was in anything other than Canadian waters. Had some subtle form of plate tectonics moved the ship? Had a renegade bureaucrat in Washington shifted the international boundary line? In the back of the courtroom people began to whisper.

It was a majestic claim. If Shannon could prove that a part of the shipwreck was in Michigan waters and the ruins were a natural resource, then he could invoke the Great Lakes Lands Act, which required the state "to preserve and protect the interests of the general public." In Shannon's mind, "preserve and protect" meant that the bell had to stay where it was, out of the reach of a rival.

Shannon's case moved inexorably toward its central theme. Again, referring to his typed notes, Michael Rizik addressed Judge Glazer.

"Mr. Shannon...has a financial interest at stake...he wants...to publish his book and documentary film...devoted to the study and exposition of the *Edmund Fitzgerald*."

Judge Glazer: "How will the project suffer financially if the defendant retrieves the ship's bell?"

Rizik: "One of the issues that Mr. Shannon is addressing in the book, Your Honor, is how the ship sank, so he wants to go down and videotape more information...the original bell missing from that ship destroys the integrity of that ship and the information that Mr. Shannon will then have to show when he does his speaking tour or when he publishes his book...If the original bell is missing, it destroys...any financial return that he may have..."

Judge Glazer: "My question is still unanswered. How does it affect the financial prospects of his enterprise?"

Rizik: "He may not sell as many books—the videotape, the documentary he does, which shows a picture of the ship without the bell, may not sell as well..."

Judge Glazer: "That's frankly a little hard for me to swallow. Do you have marketing experts...prepared to testify that the removal of the ship's bell...is going to severely detract from the financial prospects of his film, or videotape, or book, or other enterprises associated with this proposed dive?"

Michael Rizik shifted the dialogue into areas of precedent comprehended only by judges and lawyers. Then, as quickly as it had veered away, the discussion returned to the real issue. Rizik raised his voice slightly. "As [Shannon] will tell you, Judge, he sees a strong likelihood that the book may not sell as well, because he wants more photographs, and without the bell, the book may suffer. The same thing is true of the film. Believe me, Judge, this is an adversarial setting. There is no love lost between my client and Mr. Farnquist."

Love was the last thing in the minds of the two diminutive combatants. The issue here was control of the bell and its commercial potential. Both men had forgotten the lake, forgotten the storm, and forgotten the ship and her crew.

Chapter Fourteen

FIRE INSIDE THE LAKE

Lake Superior, July 4, 1995

It was noon, and five hundred feet below the surface of the lake, the roof of the *Fitzgerald* pilothouse was lit by a fluorescent fire. The light was blazing from the front of two subs that had parked their bows on the edge of the roof. The smaller sub hovered on the front railing and faced the *Fitzgerald*'s stern. The bigger sub had placed its skids gently on the starboard railing. At the intersection of their lights was the ship's bell.

The bell did not reflect the brilliant lights coming from the two subs. Over the years, its solid brass surface had been transformed by the lake into an earth-red color. Engraved across its midsection were two rows of letters, some containing the original black paint, that silently announced the name of the ship. Weighing 200 pounds and measuring 21½ inches in diameter at the base, the bell was suspended inside three steel stanchions so that its lower rim hung just above the roof. Directly in front of it was a perpendicular steel pipe that allowed its clapper to be pulled from inside the pilothouse.

Behind the bell, leaning casually against the question-mark curve of its rear stanchion, was a man in a yellow diving suit. There was nothing in the diver's demeanor to indicate that Bruce Fuoco was in the midst of a thick adrenaline moment.

Fuoco's 21st-century suit, the Newt Suit, with its pressure-resistant shell of aluminum, titanium, stainless steel, and teflon, its 20 fluid-compensating rotating joints, flexible hand manipulator system, four electric thrusters and communication and life-support systems, was working perfectly. The problem confronting Bruce Fuoco had nothing to do with his suit, but with the upcoming choreography of the bell's release.

Earlier, Fuoco had wound two thick canvas straps around the upper part of the bell's supporting stanchions and looped them into a lift line leading to the surface. Then he'd used his cutting torch to burn through the two forward stanchions and most of the third, a thick piece of channel iron. In a few minutes, when he completed the last cut through the channel iron, his teammates in the tugboat 500 feet over his head would put a serious strain on the winch that would yank the bell free of its foundation. It had to be done with quicksilver timing and speed so that the bell, with its three supporting legs, would not snag in the forest of vertical steel — the foremast and crow's nest, the radio direction finder loop, the FM and TV antennae — jutting up from the roof. If the timing and direction were off, the bell might snag or act like the butt of a felled tree, leap off its foundation, punch through Fuoco's faceplate, and bring the full weight of Lake Superior into his suit.

Bruce Fuoco was recognized as the best in his field. He was 37 years old and had spent two decades diving. Fuoco worked at an occupation whose hazards, until the development of the Newt Suit, included ruptured lungs, sinus squeeze, nitrogen narcosis, high-pressure nervous syndrome, aseptic necrosis, decompression sickness, hypothermia, and a host of other debilitating traumas. He and his support team, the six men in the blue jumpsuits on the tugboat above, the same jovial, easygoing, hard-drinking professionals who had assisted him into the suit, lowered him to this depth and were monitoring his every movement and breath, were part of a special underwater fraternity. Fuoco looked out through his faceplate at the bell and the steel pipes and beams surrounding it and decided that maybe he would have a quiet word with one of his fraternity brothers.

Doug Osbourne was inside the control van on the deck of the tug, 50 stories above Fuoco. He was standing in front of two banks of display panels that told him everything he wanted to know about the Newt Suit's performance, including internal pressure, oxygen status, and carbon dioxide levels. At that moment, Osbourne was leaning back, looking at a television monitor. Wired to a miniature camera on the Newt Suit's left shoulder, it gave him a close-up of Fuoco's left forearm and the bell hanging inside its stanchions. Osbourne reached up to adjust his black headset. He heard a faint chuckle. "Ah, Doug, you ready to pull this home?"

Osbourne glanced out the door of the control van at the stern of the tug. He could see one of the three anchor lines that held the tug in position.

"Yeah, we've already moved the vessel."

Fuoco paused and then said calmly, "When I make my last cut, I'm going to remove my manipulator with lightning speed and fly up with the bell. I don't know if I can catch it. Hopefully there won't be too many obstacles."

Osbourne's eyes swept across the display panels. He had spent thousands of hours underwater as a commercial diver, many of them in a predecessor to the Newt Suit. On one dive he had descended 300 feet below the fathom-thick ice of the North West Passage and wrested the wheel from a three-masted British bark that had been on the bottom for more than a century.

"Okay, Bruce. Remember, it's an electric winch and we can come full up on it or jog it."

"Negative. When it comes free — and you'll see it on your video monitor — you gotta come full up. Come full up for 15 feet to make sure it's clear of the RDF loop on the port side."

"Yeah," Osbourne said quietly. "We'll come up full."

A few seconds went by as their eyes fixed on the silver mirror stretching across the mouth of the bell. It told them that its interior was full of oxygen and other gases that had been discharged from Fuoco's cutting torch. It told them the bell was a bomb.

Osbourne came at the subject obliquely. "It looks like there's a little brown sludge in there," he said. Both men knew what would happen if the tip of Fuoco's burning torch came too close to the lethal mixture. The shock wave would be felt on the surface. You could feel the what-the-hell smile in Fuoco's voice. "Yeah," he said. "It's explosive."

The brass bell on the pilothouse roof.
Photo: Harbor Branch Oceanographic and Damir Chytil.

Osbourne kept glancing at the open door of the control van, wishing he could close it. Just outside, in the bright sunshine, there was a mob scene — a motley assembly of dignitaries, visitors, hangers-on, and cameramen wearing T-shirts and windbreakers and bush vests, running this way and that, stumbling over cables, yelling at each other, awash with excitement.

In the otherworldly depths below, Fuoco stared beyond the silhouette of the bell into the blinding halo of lights coming from the two subs. He could see their white outlines more clearly than a few minutes earlier. This meant that most of the sediment that had swirled up from the pilothouse roof had been carried away by the slow-moving currents. He reached down with his left manipulator, pulled its claw tight, and lifted a slender cutting rod out of its quiver. Carefully, he transferred it to his right hand and, with a series of gentle taps, locked it into the end of his cutting torch. Inside the nearest sub, a cameraman followed Fuoco's every move like a sniper, keeping him dead center of a high-resolution television frame.

Fuoco leaned toward his head mike and said softly, "Make it hot."

Osbourne reached down to a panel next to his knee and flicked a switch — a bolt of 400 amperes of electricity sped down a black wire through 500 feet of lake. At the tip of the cutting rod it slammed into a stream of high-pressure oxygen. There was a small explosion, a muffled *whaa-uump*, and then the water was burning as bright as the sun: an orange ball the size of a fist, throwing up a column of silver bubbles.

This portable Vesuvius was less than an arm's length from Fuoco's faceplate. He tensed his calves and the muscles in his right arm and slowly, very carefully, brought the fire against the starboard side of the bell's rear stanchion, trying to align it with the cut he had made earlier. The thunderlight was astonishingly bright, its temperature so hot that it created currents that lifted the rooftop sediments and churned the water into the color of coffee.

The tip of the cast-iron and magnesium cutting rod was 5,000 degrees Fahrenheit. Fuoco nudged the fire horizontally along the shank of the angle-iron, away from his suit. The polyurethane-aluminum shield on his left arm gave him some confidence, but not much. One small slip of this trembling light and there would be an unspeakable instant of recognition as the sun and then the lake rammed into his suit.

Bruce Fuoco in the Newt Suit moving the replica brass bell into position on the pilothouse roof.
Photo: Tony Chelsom

The fear of death was always with Fuoco and his fellow divers. But they talked around it, circling the subject with breezy humor, disguising it with stories about diving accidents that had happened to someone else. It helped to explain the drunken rambles that began at four on a Friday afternoon and went on until well after midnight.

"Give it a tug," said Fuoco. The lift line tightened, but the bell did not move. "Give it a tug, topside." The line went taut, slackened slightly, and then went taut again. The bell stayed where it was. Confident that he had cut through all but the last threads of steel, Fuoco had shut off the stream of oxygen and extinguished the thunderlight. The lift line jerked upward again and then suddenly went slack.

"Hang on," said Osbourne. "We just lost something on the boom." He leaned out the open door of the van to see what had happened. The television people, dignitaries, journalists, and groupies were all jabbering and craning their necks looking at the tip of a one-story-high wishbone boom hanging out over the water on the port side. Metal fittings that held a steel beam had fractured; the lift line that ran up to the beam and over a pulley was limp. A man in a blue jumpsuit began climbing up one side of the boom to inspect the damage.

Back inside the van, Osbourne adjusted his headset. "Ah, Bruce, we've got a little problem up here. The beam has come down. We've got to do a rigging job." Osbourne's heart might have been pounding, but his words drifted down through the lake as if he were commenting on a fumble in last year's Super Bowl game.

"Anybody hurt?" asked Fuoco.

"Negative," said Osbourne.

Of all the people out on the lake that day, only Fuoco and the men in the blue jumpsuits were aware of the forces that had shuddered through the lift line pointed at the sky. Fuoco leaned over to get a better look at the cut he had made. "I'm going to get another rod and do this properly," he said.

"Don't cut it off yet," said Osbourne. "We don't have a hold on it." Two blue jumpsuits were up on the boom now, hands working together, heads nodding in concert.

"It's not a good cut," said Fuoco.

"I know," laughed Osbourne. "It took my beam."

Down on the pilothouse roof, inside the thinning dust cloud, Fuoco had flexed the knees of his suit so that he could kneel and have a closer look at his incision. "Ah Doug, there's more than a few threads holding it. There's some major material here."

Fuoco detected what might have been a soft chuckle sliding down the communications line. It was time for some good ol' boy humility. "I'll make it up to you," he said. "I promise."

There was nothing more to say and so they waited in silence as the two blue jumpsuits began to work on the boom. In a lifetime of diving, the brethren had never seen anything like what had been going on in the water for the past two days. Each day they waited for the Canadian navy ship *HMCS Cormorant* to come in close to their position and drop her two subs. Then they waited until both subs found the *Fitzgerald* and positioned themselves on the rim of the pilothouse roof. This sometimes took hours. Then they waited until the lights were turned on and the cameraman was ready. If the water went cloudy, as it frequently did with so many propellers and thrusters stirring up the sediment, they had to wait some more. It was frustrating. If the subs had not been making the film for Tom Farnquist, the brethren could have cut the bell free and lifted it to the surface in a matter of minutes.

Once the beam was fixed and the lift line repositioned under the boom, Fuoco said quietly, "Make it hot," and the 400 amps went hurtling down the wire and the thunderlight came on again. Even in water the temperature of melting ice, the tip of the cutting rod burned so brightly that it hurt to look at it. This time Fuoco used up most of the full length of the cutting rod before shutting off the oxygen. He waited for a few seconds after the fire had been extinguished by the lake.

"Give it a tug," he said. The lift line jerked and then stopped. The upper part of the stanchion seemed to lean slightly. "Come on baby." Then the bell and its trio of supports were gone, yanked skyward, leaving behind a stream of spilled bubbles.

"Bingo," shouted Fuoco. "Pull me up. Pull up on the bell." He watched through the dome of his pressure suit as the bell headed for the loops of the RDF antenna, changed direction, and soared over it. Then he was up in the water beside it, checking the lift line and straps. "The slings are all right," he said. "We are clear."

Then Fuoco and the bell began a slow ascent through the blackness of the lake. They climbed up together past the crow's nest and the iron tip of the foremast, leaving the subs with their lights still blazing below. For long minutes they were alone inside the cold, barely a few arm's lengths apart, the great waters spinning them in a slow, lazy spiral.

The crowd on the deck of the tugboat heard that the bell had been cut free and began to murmur and shuffle around, looking for just the right camera angle so that when the bell broke through the surface into the sunlight they could capture the perfect Kodak moment. There were so many of them jammed against the railing on the port side that the tug had a faint list.

The surface of the lake was now crawling with boats. One of them, an 80-foot yacht called the *Northlander*, carried wives, mothers, sisters, brothers, sons, and daughters of the *Fitzgerald*'s crew. A few minutes earlier, they had placed wreaths, including a large green one with 29 intertwined roses, upon the water. For the Hudsons, Armagosts, Rozmans, Champeaus, and the others, being out here — *where it happened* — was another step in the search for meaning. Their men had died far away and without a grave. There had been no flag-draped coffin, no interment. More than anything, they wanted some evidence that their men had lived and worked. They looked across the lake, at the spot where the bell was to come up, trying to understand a tragedy that had for most of them contained far too many troubling aspects. But at last they were together, as one "family," participating in something that resembled closure.

One of them, Jack Champeau, had transferred to the tugboat so that when the bell was placed on deck he could say a few words on behalf of the families. Champeau stood under the haze pouring out of the diesel

Bruce Fuoco watching the bell being raised from the water.   Photo: Doug Elsey

generators' exhaust pipe and thought of his brother Buck, the *Fitzgerald*'s third engineer. In 1969, when Jack shipped out to Vietnam, Buck had taken him aside and told him that if he was killed in action he would do everything he could to bring back his body for burial in America. In 1975, when Buck was killed by Lake Superior, Jack vowed to do everything he could to recover his older brother's body. Jack looked across

The bell on the deck of the tugboat.   Photo: Doug Elsey

the deck at the men in blue jumpsuits. He now knew how unforgiving the lake was and what it had done to the ship and that he would never bring his brother home. But recovering the bell was the next best thing. In a few minutes, when the bell was securely on deck, he would share some of these thoughts publicly in a short, moving speech.

As the bell was lifted clear of the sparkling surface of the lake, water slid, like a shower of silver, down its flanks. A delicious tremor ran through the crowd. The air buzzed, hummed, clicked, and whirred as a hundred Nikons, Minoltas, Olympuses, and Sonys took aim and fired.

Chapter Fifteen

BLUE CASINO

Two days after the dives to salvage the *Fitzgerald*'s bell, a banquet to celebrate its recovery was held in downtown Sault Ste. Marie. The banquet hall was located inside a recently erected sprawl of low-roofed buildings called the Keewadin Casino. To get to it, the guests walked through a large glass door into a blaze of lights. In the foyer, they were met by a trio of security guards. Then they turned right, walked down a short, dark hallway, and stepped through a wide, rectangular opening. The banquet room contained rows of white linen–covered tables sparkling under simulated candlelight. The room was alive with chatter. It had blown hard and cold off the big lake all day and everyone was happy to be inside, where warmth was being dispensed from bottles of Bacardi and Captain Morgan.

At the far end of the room, a crowd of people had gathered around the *Fitzgerald*'s bell. It stood on a raised platform inside an aluminum pipe frame. Photographs of some of the lost crewmen had been placed next to it.

The guest list included many of the families of the lost crewmen, the full complement of officers and crew from *HMCS Cormorant*, and several hundred others. On one side of the room, at the end of a table, John McCarthy was describing how his father, Jack, had carried out his duties as first mate on the *Fitzgerald*. "Jack was a perfectionist," he said. "And very adept in his use of words. He used them to tell jokes, issue commands, and swear sweetly when he needed to. He had a wonderful sense of humor and his men loved him for it."

It was warm in the room. McCarthy had taken off his jacket. He was wearing a red-and-white-striped shirt and a necktie. A line of moisture appeared on his forehead. He was asked if he knew his father's old friend, Captain McSorley. McCarthy thought for a moment and shifted in his chair. "McSorley was an enigma," he said. "A very private and very intense man. It was almost impossible to know what he was thinking. But Jack knew. And Jack helped him communicate with his crew. I think McSorley needed Jack to translate his silences."

John McCarthy's four summers working on the big ships had given him some insight into the floating world where the air outside was always clean and the men were free to exist inside the hard work and unpredictable events that could harm them. It was part of the legacy handed down to all lake sailors.

John McCarthy was 30 years old when the accident happened. He was now fifty, the vice-president of an insurance brokerage company and living in Cleveland not far from the house where he grew up. He exuded decency. "Jack loved the daily challenge of getting things done. And getting them done right. He was a fixer. McSorley made the hard decisions, but Jack inspired the men to do the work."

There was a question that McCarthy's companion did not have the courage to ask: How had the son dealt with the nightmare of his father's final moments? How had he wrestled with the thoughts of those last seconds, when there is green water foaming through the windows and legs that won't hold you? The person looking into McCarthy's eyes for the answer had spent years at sea. He sensed that McCarthy took comfort from his family and friends and memories and the old rule of the sea that men take care of each other, no matter what. Somehow, John McCarthy knew that as the ship was being pulled under, his father and Ernest McSorley would have been working together, shoulder to shoulder.

John McCarthy took off his rimless glasses, wiped his forehead, and began to talk to his brother, Danny, and his sister, Beth. The three heads bent together, the cadence of love in their voices joining them. Before their father disappeared, death was an abstraction. Then, the accident had cruelly disrupted the natural order of their family. It had vanished, and with it the warmth of a man who complained about the weather, sang in the shower, and filled a room with his laughter. It was this that they shared with the other members of the *Fitzgerald* family. For 20 years the families of 29 crewmen had been living with death's terrible finality and the havoc it wreaked. The accident had injured them, but it had not stilled their love or memories.

As they were talking, a short man with narrow shoulders drifted in behind them and began talking to the people at the next table. Tom Farnquist's face was impassive. There was no reading it any more than a sandbar exposed at low tide.

Farnquist began to talk quietly into an older man's ear. The hint of a smile flashed across his face. Farnquist finally had the ship's bell, the very soul of the *Fitzgerald*, within his grasp. For Farnquist, the bell was vibrant with commercial possibilities. His building, designed for it, would be filled with photographs and display cases. In the years to come, he would construct a movie theater next door. Thousands of people would open their wallets to see the bell and the big-screen movie about how it was recovered from the pilothouse roof of the *Fitzgerald*. And then he would usher all those people into his new gift shop.

The best-kept secret of the entire project was that Farnquist had acquired the footage for his movie at a fraction of its real cost. In return for pictures for a magazine article, *National Geographic* had contributed tens of thousands of dollars. Inspired by the technical challenge of film-ing underwater, Sony had loaned several hundred thousand dollars of high-definition television equipment. But the mother lode, the real bonanza, came out of the pockets of the Canadian taxpayer. Under fire from a national scandal in Somalia, and eager for some positive public-ity, the Department of National Defence agreed to donate *HMCS Cormorant*, her 90-man crew, and her two subs for 10 days of diving—at a cost estimated to be in the range of $400,000.

Now that he had his film and the *Fitzgerald*'s bell had been officially transferred from the province of Ontario to the state of Michigan and then to his museum, Farnquist would recast himself as the fierce guard-ian of the site. For years he had been clamoring to dive the *Fitzgerald*; from this day forward he would work furiously to prevent others from doing so. Sensing the hypocrisy, one perceptive critic would write: "The presentation of the bell to the victims' relatives garnered much publicity and was a considerate gesture, but in truth the bell remains under the direct control and possession of the party responsible for salvaging it.

That same party, while using the wreck for personal and professional gain is now attempting to prevent others from doing the same. Having thoroughly explored the *Fitzgerald* wreck site and taken everything from photographs to a rare artifact, his position now is 'let's get the media and the victims' relatives to pressure the Canadian Government into declaring the wreck a grave site, off-limits to further explorations.' "

From somewhere in the banquet hall a voice rose out of the crowd like a spike being hammered into the ceiling. It belonged to Emory Kristof, a big-boned, black-bearded photographer who had been Farnquist's collaborator in putting the bell-raising deal together. One reason Kristof spoke with such gusto was that he was partially deaf from years of diving. Another was that he was always trying to make a point — his point — to the person he was talking to. Possessing extraordinary talents and an uncensored hubris, Kristof was driven by the demands of his own self-interest.

Kristof had organized the gritty details for Farnquist, including the Canadian navy diving-support vessel, its 90-man crew, its two subs, the 10 days of diving, and the precision timing of all the underwater activities. While the swarm of people on ships above the wreck site were shooting away with their little film and video cameras, Kristof was deep inside the lake scooping up the big-money images and locking them inside a black video-recording box inside the biggest of the two subs. The box weighed about a hundred pounds and boasted flashing lights, digital read-outs, and a pair of wide-body video reels. A sheath of black cables linked it into an equally ominous-looking television camera hanging at the nodal point of the sub's transparent bow. With its externally mounted rack of Hollywood sun-guns and more than half a million dollars' worth of Sony high-definition television equipment inside its pressure hull, Kristof had turned the Canadian navy sub into the world's most expensive camera housing.

The high-definition television pictures of the bow and the stern of the *Fitzgerald*, especially the images of Bruce Fuoco burning off the old bell and replacing it with a new one, were worth a fortune. They were the first-ever high-definition images taken in deep water. They could be converted into a *National Geographic* photo spread. They could be made into high-ticket photographs and posters. They could be sold as part of a one-hour television special. They could be edited into a pay-per-view theater release or marketed as a home video. The commercial possibilities were endless. It was no wonder then that Kristof and Farnquist were enjoying a sweet moment of financial bliss.

When the banquet was over, women in colorful dresses, men in jackets and ties, naval uniforms, open-necked shirts, and blue jeans moved slowly toward the door. John McCarthy and his sister, Beth, and brother, Danny, fell into step behind Captain Don Erickson, the former master of the *William Clay Ford*. Erickson was the last hero of the story, the man who had looked into the mad eye of the lake and decided he would risk everything in an attempt to find the *Fitzgerald*'s crew. The crowd surged forward and then stopped. Tom Farnquist was only a few shoulders away from Emory Kristof. Both men were smiling. At least for Kristof, the rules of the game were simple. You took what you wanted and apologized later if you were caught. Money was more important than loyalty. The crowd began to move forward again. Fred Leete was there and Bruce Fuoco and Ruth Hudson and Janice Armagost and Jack and Tom Champeau. The crowd contained those who had participated in the tragedy in a real and meaningful way. It also contained those who had finessed it into a financial enterprise.

The crowd flowed past the long white table where Farnquist's people were hawking the last of the T-shirts, sweatshirts, posters, and coffee mugs. As the crowd moved up the steps and into the dark hall beyond, it heard a faint whirring and clicking. It was the sound of money moving. The Keewadin Casino was operated by the Chippewa Indians, who had given Farnquist a two-hundred-thousand-dollar interest-free loan to finance his bell-recovery project.

The Keewadin Casino, open 24 hours a day, 365 days a year, offered its players more than one hundred thousand square feet of Vegas-style gambling with blackjack, roulette, and more than two thousand slot machines. There were hundreds of people in the Keewadin Casino this night, all working on their version of the American dream. Casino owners have a saying. "The only way to make money out of gambling is to own the place where the gambling is." It was a lesson not lost on Tom Farnquist. The only way to make money on the bell was to own the place where the bell is.

The crowd thinned and then dispersed so that only the earth-red bell, hanging in its temporary cradle, was left at the far end of the room.

It had 17 years of service to a great ship within it. It had the storm within it. And the sinking. And 20 years of lying in the darkness of an ancient lake. It had the memories of the men within it, and now the hearts of the families. Earlier that evening more than one person had approached it quietly, stared into its gleamless face, and wished it could rest within the spiritual peace of Mariners' Church.

Chapter Sixteen

TWENTY YEARS LATER

November 10, 1995

The last light from another gray November day was sliding out of the sky. Along the northern shore of Lake Superior, freezing rain and sleet pelted down out of low-lying clouds. Far away, on the southern shore, rain came down intermittently, in thin black curtains.

It was 20 years to the day that the *Fitzgerald* had vanished. Moving pinpricks of red and green lights showed where big steel ships were crossing the wide expanse of the lake. Inside, men threaded their way through passageways, surrounded by the familiar hum of machinery. Other men stood in pilothouses, looking out through the large square windows that framed the rapidly darkening sky. Behind them, fathometers flickered, radars scanned, and consoles hummed. On a few of the ships, men turned to each other and spoke quietly about the long-ago event. Some of the older men went out to the wing bridge and leaned against the railing to contemplate the great waters slipping past.

For most of those who thought about it, the "why" of the *Fitzgerald* sinking no longer seemed relevant. It was buried under 20 years of conflicting explanations and the cold weight of the lake. But, occasionally, a sailor would ask himself how a ship the size of a 72-story building could sink so quickly. Some mariners compare the *Fitzgerald* and the *Titanic*. Both ships were big and considered by many to be "unsinkable." Both sank in cold water, breaking in two and scattering their interiors and cargo across a wide area.

During the 1991 expedition to study the *Titanic* and film it in IMAX, we recovered a piece of her hull the size of a small dinner plate. At a

Canadian government laboratory in Ottawa it was analyzed for composition, corrosion, microstructure, and mechanical properties. Because the steel had a higher-than-normal sulphur content, it was extremely brittle. When the *Titanic* struck the iceberg, her hull plates did not bend, they shattered.

Each year, somewhere on the world's oceans, some two dozen cargo ships sink for reasons that defy explanation. Some marine architects believe brittle failure of the hull plates may be a contributing factor. Recently, Canadian and American experts have wondered if, at the height of the storm, a similar fate befell the *Fitzgerald*. It is a question that may only be answered when a sample of the hull is examined for its mechanical properties and microscopic structure.

On that gray November day 20 years to the day after the *Fitzgerald* vanished, a line of cars and pickup trucks made their way into the parking lot of the Thomas Edison Inn at the south end of Lake Huron. High overhead, a line of tractor-trailers inched their way across the black silhouette of the Blue Water Bridge, over the Saint Clair River. Inside, the twentieth anniversary *Edmund Fitzgerald* Memorial dinner was beginning. Some 400 people, drinks in hand, were making their way from the Hunt Lounge to the Cambridge Hall banquet room. There was a sense of expectation in the air.

The Invocation was given by Father Thomas Johnson, the pastor of Saint Christopher's Church, who spoke briefly and closed with the words "Reunite us all in the harbour of light and peace..."

After Father Johnson left the podium, the big room filled with the murmur of voices. One of them belonged to "Red" Burgner, a cook who had served nine years on the *Fitzgerald*. Two others belonged to Tom and Jack Champeau. Some of the people in the room were scuba divers with an interest in shipwrecks. Others were lawyers and businessmen with their wives. All of them were fascinated by an event they did not understand and a man who said he would explain it to them.

One of the speakers was Todd Cooper, the son of Bernie Cooper, captain of the *Arthur M. Anderson*. Cooper talked of his father's courage and pioneering spirit. He talked about holding the *Anderson*'s logbook in his hand and reading the November 10, 1975, entries made by his father. Although taller, Todd Cooper had the same facial features as the man who reached safety and then turned his ship around to search for a fellow captain and his crew. Cooper spoke with honesty and conviction, telling his audience that seven hours earlier, before the rain clamped down, the *Arthur M. Anderson*, fully laden, had steamed down the Saint Clair River within 200 yards of where they were sitting.

In the narrow hallway outside the banquet room, a long table had been set up and covered with a green felt cloth. Behind it three women were unpacking cardboard boxes. The contents of the boxes were carefully arranged in piles along the table. Next to the last pile, one of the women placed a small gray machine that imprinted Visa cards.

Inside the room, Frederick Joseph Shannon was speaking. Master of ceremonies and the organizer of tonight's event, Shannon was wearing gray flannels, a dark safari jacket, and a rose-colored shirt. His black tie had a hand-painted portrait of the *Fitzgerald* on it, bow on, steaming straight at the viewer.

Speaking into the paired microphones in front of him, Shannon introduced some of the members of his 1994 expedition. "Ric Mixter, videographer … Chris Chabot, screenwriter … Steve Harrington, legal adviser…. And my wife, Betty, who was the cook on the project." Dark-haired and smiling, Betty stepped in from the hallway, where she was unpacking the boxes. The audience turned and applauded.

Shannon continued to talk in sentences that were an odd mixture of hubris and humility. At times, when he paused for breath, the audience tensed, perhaps wondering if he was going to launch into one of his famous diatribes against Tom Farnquist and the Shipwreck Society. The notes on the back page of tonight's program hinted that he might. They read: "It was indeed a sad day in maritime history when an army of more than 100 salvers … raped the ship of her soul, the … pilothouse bell. If these people are allowed to continue removing artifacts … it will destroy the efforts of hundreds of concerned citizens who fought to establish underwater preserves so that we might pass along our heritage to a new generation." Shannon knew that what he had written was not completely true, but the words remained on the page, unexplored.

Eight hours earlier, at his wood-frame museum in Whitefish Point, Tom Farnquist had engineered his own version of the twentieth anniversary.

The sky was overcast and the ground covered with a thin shroud of snow. As the great lake brooded in the background, some one hundred people crowded into the museum's tiny exhibit room. There were chairs for about 30 of the next of kin; the other guests stood quietly around the periphery. There were speeches and prayers. Cheryl Rozman, the daughter of Ray Ransom Cundy, spoke briefly about how much the recovery of the bell meant to the *Fitzgerald* families. Farnquist, wearing a dark suit and tie and a white shirt, talked about how challenging it had been to bring the bell to the surface. His words came out smoothly; they offered no hint of his personal agenda.

As he spoke, Farnquist stood beside the bell. Since it had been recovered from the lake it had gone through two major transformations. At Michigan State University, a team of hard-working conservators had carefully restored it to its original condition. Over a period of six weeks, it was mechanically and chemically cleaned. Then it was coated with six layers of lacquer. When it arrived at his museum, Farnquist took one look and decided he did not like its appearance. Without consulting the *Fitzgerald* families or the good people at Michigan State, he took the bell to an antique-furniture restorer and had it sanded and polished to give it a deep gleam. This caused concern among some of the family members. What had been whispered about Farnquist's rule-bending behavior seemed to have been confirmed. The families were also dismayed about what they had heard concerning the taconite pellets. Farnquist knew that the Ontario government's archeological licence stated that the bell was the only object to be removed from the ship. But he had obtained some of the *Fitzgerald*'s cargo, and was passing out the marble-sized pellets to friends.

Outside the banquet room at the Thomas Edison Inn, down the hall from the long green table laden with merchandise, three people were stacking color flyers and cost sheets on a table set up beside a row of easels. Recessed lights from the ceiling burned down on seven large paintings of the *Fitzgerald*. The color prints, and the accompanying ink-print set, showed five underwater views of the forward part of the ship, one view of the overturned stern section and one showing the two sections and the shattered break between them. As one and then two people came in to take a closer look at the prints, a woman in a black dress placed a credit card machine at one end of the table.

In the banquet room the lights were dimmed and two large video screens came to life. Chairs were brought in closer to tables and men leaned forward on their elbows. This was what they had come for, this is what Frederick Joseph Shannon had advertised in his brochure, this is what they were each paying forty dollars to see. "The truth as it has never before been revealed.... One man's personal twelve-year quest... dramatic new evidence...the egos, politics and influences guiding past expeditions...what happened during the last minutes...the location of the missing crewmen...the mysterious area of human remains..."

The body. It was Shannon's trump card in his ongoing battle with Tom Farnquist. Farnquist had his bell, but Shannon had his body. At least the exclusive footage of it. His pronouncements about the body lying in the sediment near the port side of the bow appalled most people and raised the ire of Michigan congressman Bart Stupak, who said: "I believe Mr. Shannon's intentions are immoral and tasteless. It appears his only motive to display these pictures is to make a profit."

This was an issue that touched everyone. A dead body is a reminder of our own mortality. A horrible death brings together the two things we fear most—unrestrained aggression and thoughts of our own death. Every human body, even a lifeless one lying at the bottom of a lake, informs us about a universal truth. And without knowing it, Shannon had stumbled on that universal truth. His mistake was to try to take personal advantage of it.

In the rain-filled shadows under the Blue Water Bridge a freighter was midcurrent, heading north. It was too dark to see the ship's name on her stern, but in the lights struggling out from shore it was possible to see the pilothouse fronted with its wall of windows. Inside were maps and chart tables, consoles of electronic equipment, radars, and vigilant men completing the complicated task of piloting their ship up the Saint Clair River into the black slab of Lake Huron.

The 400 people who'd paid forty dollars to have dinner and see pictures of the fallen *Fitzgerald* sailor were disappointed. What Frederick Shannon showed on the screen was 15 minutes edited from his 50-minute home video. The scenes flowed by quickly: the lake, the ship, the little submarine, the interviews, the submerged steel ruins, and a few seconds of something lying on the lake floor. Was it a body? Even for the doctor sitting next to Jack Champeau, it was hard to say. About halfway through the video, Tom Champeau got up and left the room. It was impossible to know if he left in disgust, or because his knees were sore. His brother, Jack, stayed seated until the video screens flickered to black and then to blue snow. Throughout, Jack had been looking at the screen in front of him as if trying to divine a way to bring home his long-lost brother.

The audience rose and began moving toward the open doors. Fred Shannon walked slowly across the front of the room, shaking hands and smiling. Jack Champeau followed the crowd inching out the middle door. In the hallway, people were jammed tight against the long green table, confronted by piles of blue and white ball caps, navy blue coffee mugs, and off-white T-shirts—all inscribed with the Shannon Expedition logo. The crowd was trapped between the table and a blue board listing the prices: Coffee Mugs, $8.00; Ball Caps, $8.00; 20th Anniversary T-shirts, $13.00; Expedition '94 T-shirts, $28.00; Site Maps, Small $8.00, Large, $25.00. The video was available for $49.50. Farther down the hall, the crowd was stalled by another display. "Color Print Artist Proofs $950. Set of Seven Color Prints $699. Set of Seven Pen and Ink Prints $249." The seven original paintings could be purchased for $37,100 each. If all the paintings, artists proofs, color prints, and pen-and-ink prints were sold, their total value would be more than a million dollars. The promotional flyers contained the words "We welcome layaways." One of the ironies of modern culture is that the moment something is deemed genuine, mysterious, and grand—whether that something is a shipwreck or its bell—money flies to it, hollows it out, and transforms it.

Jack and Tom Champeau left the confined spaces where the cash was going into the till and walked through the carpeted foyer to the front door. For a few minutes, they stood together under a black sky full of uncontained energies. They knew that they could not travel back in time and restore the beloved face that had disappeared in a storm 20 years ago. Each had found the strength that never fails, the strength to accept what cannot be changed. In their own way, both men had come to terms with that long, dark night.

Chapter Seventeen

THE HONOR GUARD

On Sunday, November 12, 1995, inside Mariners' Church in Detroit, Father Richard Ingalls led the twentieth-anniversary *Edmund Fitzgerald* Memorial Service. Every pew was filled with loyal parishioners and surviving families of the lost crewmen. They included the Champeaus, the Cundys, the Hudsons, the McCarthys, the Riipas, and the Waltons. The right-hand side of the church held several rows of older men and two women wearing navy blue uniforms emblazoned with gold braid and service ribbons.

Each year, on the first Sunday in November, Father Ingalls held a service to remember the crew of the *Edmund Fitzgerald* and to honor all men and women who had died on the lakes. For the first five years the service was unpublicized because, Father Ingalls said, "We didn't want to invade the privacy of the families." With the enduring popularity of Gordon Lightfoot's song and its reference to the "Maritime Sailors' Cathedral," what was private soon became public.

As the congregation heard the first sound high above them, they rose as one and listened. It was the Brotherhood Bell ringing out as it had 20 years earlier, a sound that vaulted from building to building, now clear, now faint. They stood perfectly still listening to a sound that gave voice to deep longing.

The Lord is in his Holy Temple: Let all the earth keep silence before him...
before the service, speak to the Lord; during the service let the Lord speak to
you ...

Then came the organ music that stirred every heart, the rolling stanzas of the Mariners' Hymn, with everyone's voices, from sea cadets to ship-masters, singing the words in unison.

> *Eternal Father, strong to save*
> *Whose arm hath bound the restless wave*
> *Who bidd'st the mighty ocean deep*
> *Its own appointed limits keep;*
> *O hear us when we cry to thee*
> *For those in peril on the sea. . .*

> *Guard us O God, Almighty King,*
> *From gale of fall and fog of spring,*
> *O keep us safe from shoal and reef,*
> *Protect us on the inland seas.*
> *To long boats passing through the night,*
> *Please give the guidance of thy light*

The young voices sang with the exuberance of youth. The old voices sang with the knowledge of a world that contained the tremendous forces of its own unpredictability.

It was a comfort to be standing together, especially for those in the navy blue uniforms with the gold braid. They were captains, commanders, and an admiral in the United States Coast Guard and Great Lakes masters from the International Ship Masters' Association. There was a rhythm to the service—the Epistle, the Twenty-third Psalm, the Holy Gospel, the Offertory Anthem—that reminded them of life on board when the hours were strung together by the ringing of bells and the routines that followed.

Father Ingalls directed the service with the confidence of a captain who knew the character of his vessel and crew. He spoke quietly but with authority. The rows of people standing in front of him and the men they were remembering were faint tracings on the surface of a large mystery. The mystery included the strangeness of creation, the uncertainty of death, the elusiveness of free will, the enchantment of dreams, and the follies of human behavior.

As the burial sentences were chanted by the choir, the distinguished men and women in the navy uniforms rose from their pews and began to move toward the front of the church. Many were in their seventies or eighties. Some walked slowly, as if favoring a leg or hip. One by one, they filed up to the sanctuary until they were assembled in three rows on both sides of Father Ingalls. On a table in front of them was a large encased model of the *Edmund Fitzgerald* and below it a wreath of red roses and white carnations.

Between them, these ship captains and Coast Guard officers had served for hundreds of years on the Great Lakes and high seas. Typical of their strength and spirit was Captain Morgan L. Howell. Howell had been going to sea since 1922. He'd captained some of the most prestigious vessels on the Great Lakes and he'd sailed corvettes and minesweepers across the North Atlantic during the dark days of the Second World War. And he had been piloting an oceangoing vessel on Lake Superior on the same night the *Fitzgerald* went down. His close friend John Poviach had been at the wheel of the doomed ship. "Poviach was the best wheelsman I ever had," he said, pausing. "I was surviving while my buddy was sinking."

Captain Howell had attended all previous *Fitzgerald* memorial services, but was not among the men now standing in the sanctuary. At the last minute he had responded to a call to duty as captain of a Great

The uniformed Honor Guard at Mariners' Church.   Photo: Alan Kamuda

Laker. His fellow captains missed him because he enriched the air with his stories and made them feel young. Captain Morgan Howell was just eight years shy of being one hundred years old.

Once again the organ boomed its opening notes. The congregation stood and their voices rose as one for the recessional hymn.

The words of the memorial service carried some of the families to the big lake, where the elements met and the sky and the water went black and time and eternity splintered. Their sons and husbands and brothers had been out there 20 years earlier, cut down like God's own sweet hay.

There were abiding mysteries. Did God have a hand in this? Or was this a world with a holy fire in the sky, all power and brilliance and beauty and no meaning? What was to be made of the fury of the ancient lake and the bones entombed within it? The families and members of the congregation looked at the rows of men and women in uniform and listened intently to the quiet man in the white and gold robes who spoke to them with such sincerity. And they yielded to the idea that God's unending mercy—love, loss, and redemption—was in the words and the music and the windows of this stone church.

Captain James A. Wilson was among the older men standing next to Father Ingalls. His hair was whiter than when he had been a member of the Board of Inquiry but his green eyes still gazed at far horizons. As much as anyone in the church, Jim Wilson knew that the *Fitzgerald* was a memorial to impermanence. Three years earlier he had addressed the following words to this same congregation:

"Sailors are fortunate in the gifts they receive. They have a respect and love for their fellow seafarers unknown in other careers...a respect that goes beyond the bounds of language...they have a love for the sea, lakes and the oceans....The sailor faces the everyday challenges of loneliness and separation. He faces the forces of nature...and the insufferable heat of the engine room in midsummer...finally there is the storm ...the one that tests the mettle and abilities of everyone involved...the skill of the master...the performance of the crew....The mariners present know that the *Fitzgerald*'s storm could have been their storm. No one knows that better than Captain Erickson..."

On this November Sunday, Captain Don Erickson was standing on the right side of Father Ingalls, the crown of his head barely topping the reverend's chin. His blue, 67-year-old eyes looked up at the White

Ensign of the Royal Navy hanging on the gospel side of the nave. Three rows of service ribbons were clamped to his chest. Four glittering lines of braid wrapped the base of each sleeve. His hands were gently clasped in front of his uniform, port over starboard.

Like the other old salts that flanked him, Erickson's mind kept drifting from the church to the lake, a familiar journey made in an instant and without effort. He saw the *Fitzgerald*'s men in his mind's eye as he had seen them so many times, positioned throughout the ship, knowing it was going to happen. Probably 10 of them forward and 19 aft. Four in the pilothouse and four in the engine room, with the rest sitting together in the lounge and galley. The lake had compressed them into an understanding so close it approached an epiphany.

First came the awesome angle. The great ship shimmying beneath them. Then a sliding, a rushing forward into thunder, the air around them filled with things coming loose. They would be breathing hard when the water came to them and then into them, drawing the fire from their lungs. The men in the pilothouse would have gone quickly. For the men in the stern, it would have been slower as the great shanks of steel shuddered and the spine of the ship snapped and began to disintegrate, the stern and its engine room rolling like the earth turning, the floor climbing unbelievably over their heads.

Erickson knew this and tried not to think about it just as he had tried not to think about it that night. The only thing on his mind that night had been to muster his own will and the will of his crew and get his ship out of sheltered waters and into the storm just in case someone was floating out there in the darkness. He had known some of those men. He had known that if the ship didn't kill them the waves would, and if the waves hadn't, the cold would, but as long as there was the slightest chance of a miracle, he would be there holding up his end of the bargain. It was the mariners' code and it was all about fidelity. Fidelity to duty and honor. Fidelity under bright flares falling from rescue planes and a black universe of contending furies.

Erickson had discovered there are depths in a lake that no one knows about. You go about the daily life aboard ship, you eat your breakfast, you read the sky and sign the logbook, you move through your whole career, and you never know what real fear tastes like. But one night the lake become huge and black and you experience something that reaches down to your very soul. Twenty years later you are still thinking about it. You finally understand that instability lies at the heart of the world.

The church fell silent and then filled with a woman's voice singing Gordon Lightfoot's "Wreck of the Edmund Fitzgerald." There was another silence and from inside the church the sound of a bell tolling. The congregation and the families and the distinguished mariners listened as the names of the 29 sailors were spoken and the Memorial Bell was rung and was echoed by the Brotherhood Bell in the tower.

There wasn't anyone in the congregation who didn't feel fortunate to be alive and in this sacred place with these majestic men and women standing in front of them. Everyone remembering. No one felt more blessed than Ruth Hudson, who stepped forward to ring the Memorial Bell when her son's name was called. Seven months after Bruce was killed, his beautiful daughter, Heather, was born. Six years later, her mother married a wonderful man. Heather, now 20 years old and in her second year at college, had Bruce's dark hair and deep-set eyes. At today's service, Ruth and Oddis and Heather and her parents were held together by their love for each other and the young man who loved the big ships and his blue Kawasaki.

There wasn't anyone in the Honor Guard who hadn't lived through moments when the world changed in an instant and a life was lost and other lives had to be reconstructed slowly. They were men and women who knew that surviving such experiences meant building walls that kept even those who were closest from getting through. They also knew that such walls had to be taken down in the unending search for compassion.

The distinguished mariners were immensely practical men. They were not poets. But by stepping inside this old stone church and participating in this service, they confirmed what poet John Donne had said nearly four centuries ago.

No man is an island, intire of it selfe
any man's death diminishes me, because I am involved in mankinde
therefore never send to know for whom the bell tolls;
it tolls for thee

THE CREW OF THE *S.S. EDMUND FITZGERALD*
LOST WITH ALL HANDS, LAKE SUPERIOR,
NOVEMBER 10, 1975

McSorley, Ernest Michael	Master
McCarthy, John Henkle	First Mate
Pratt, James A.	Second Mate
Armagost, Michael Eugene	Third Mate
Holl, George John	Chief Engineer
Bindson, Edward Francis	First Assistant Engineer
Edwards, Thomas E.	Second Assistant Engineer
Haskell, Russell George	Second Assistant Engineer
Champeau, Oliver J.	Third Assistant Engineer
Beetcher, Frederick J.	Porter
Bentsen, Thomas	Oiler
Borgeson, Thomas Dale	Able-Bodied Maintenance Man
Church, Nolan Frank	Porter
Cundy, Ransom Edward	Watchman
Hudson, Bruce Lee	Deckhand
Kalmon, Allen George	Second Cook
MacLellan, Gordon F.	Wiper
Mazes, Joseph William	Special Maintenance Man
O'Brien, Eugene William	Wheelsman
Peckol, Karl Anthony	Watchman
Poviach, John Joseph	Wheelsman
Rafferty, Robert Charles	Temporary Steward (First Cook)
Riipa, Paul M.	Deckhand
Simmons, John David	Wheelsman
Spengler, William J.	Watchman
Thomas, Mark Andrew	Deckhand
Walton, Ralph Grant	Oiler
Weiss, David Elliot	Cadet (deck)
Wilhelm, Blaine Howard	Oiler

ACKNOWLEDGMENTS

This book is dedicated to the *Fitzgerald* families, who gave me my first real view of the meaning of the tragedy, and to Harbor Branch Oceanographic Institution, who gave me my first view of the wreckage.

The cooperation of the *Fitzgerald* families was as heart-warming as it was essential and I would like especially to thank John, Dan, and Beth (Blassucci) McCarthy, Ruth and Oddis Hudson, Jack, Tom, and Mary (Soying) Champeau, Janice, Michele, and Christopher Armagost, and Cheryl Rozman.

My thanks to Rick Herman, Tim Askew, and the hard-working crew of the *Edwin Link* and the research sub *Clelia*.

To David Conklin, for his splendid illustrations.

Thanks to Jack Leitch, Captain Kevin Kelly, Alex Eliot, and all the others at Upper Lakes Shipping who made my trip on the *Seaway Queen* and to the Port Weller Drydocks so informative. And to Tony Chesterman, Ray Johnston, and Captain John Pace at Canada Steamship Lines for their encouragement. And to Steve Lapczak and Mike Leduc and the others at Environment Canada who helped me understand the dynamics of the November storm.

And a tip of the hat to Phil Nuytten, Doug Elsey, Bruce Fuoco, Doug Osbourne, and the Newt Suit team for their patience, professionalism, and humor.

To Fred Stonehouse and Robert Hemming for writing such informative books. To Ed Clark, Dianne Smith-Sanderson, and the team at Canada Trust for their support. And to Tony Fredo at Ford of Canada, and Jackie Famulak at Apple Canada, for their assistance.

To Bob Graham at the Institute for Great Lakes Research, Bowling Green State University, John Polacsek at the Dossin Great Lakes Museum, Pat Labadie at the Canal Park Marine Museum, and Ken Vrana at the Center for Maritime and Underwater Resource Management, for helping me with the historical aspects of the story.

And Captain Fred Leete, Captain Janet Provost Cummings, Captain Jimmie Hobaugh, Captain Don Erickson, and Captain Ratch Wallace for aligning my nautical compass.

To Father Richard Ingalls and Gordon Lightfoot for their enduring insights. To Barry Harvey at Moose Music Ltd. And to Lara, Jordan, and Debbie for their enduring patience.

To Alison Maclean, Nicole de Montbrun, and the team at Macmillan Canada.

And Susan Bassett-Klauber, Damir Chytil, Mark Harper, Bob Kutzleb, Bob Campbell, Peter Engelbert, John Halsey, Renee L. Cowdrey, Mrs. Elizabeth Cutler, Jim Sward, Michael Boothman, Pat Brigham, Teddy Tucker, Adrian Hooper, Martha Howarth, and the team at BGM.

BIBLIOGRAPHY

Coles, William, *A History of Old Mariners' Church*, Detroit, Michigan.

Cooper, Captain Jesse B., Speech at Wisconsin Marine Historical Society, Milwaukee, November 7, 1986

Cutler, Elizabeth and Hurthe, Walter (1983) *Six Fitzgerald Brothers — Lake Captains All*. Wisconsin Marine Historical Society, Milwaukee.

Eichenlaub, Val (1995) *Weather and Climate of the Great Lakes Region*. The University of Notre Dame Press, South Bend, Indiana.

Hemming, Robert J. (1981) *Gales of November*. Thunder Bay Press, Holt, Michigan, reprinted and revised, 1997.

Hind, John Anthony (1965) *Background to Ship Design and Ship Building Production*. Temple Press Books

Lee, Robert E. (1977) *Edmund Fitzgerald 1957-1975*. Great Lakes Maritime Institute, Michigan.

Noel, Captain John V. (1960) *Knight's Modern Seamanship*. D. Van Nostrand Co., New York, New York.

Saunders, Catherine M. (1992) *Surviving Grief... and Learning to Live Again*. John Wiley and Sons, Inc., New York, New York.

Stadler, Michael (1987) *Psychology of Sailing*. Highmark Publishing Ltd.

Stonehouse, Frederick (1995) *The Wreck of the Edmund Fitzgerald*. Thunder Bay Press, Holt, Michigan

U.S. Coast Guard Investigation Report July, 1977. *S. S. Edmund Fitzgerald Marine Casualty Report*, Washington, D.C.

Van Dorn, William G. (1974) *Oceanography and Seamanship*. Dodd, Mead and Co., New York, New York.

Wilson, James, *Address At Mariners' Church*. November 8, 1992

Wolff, Julius F., Jr. (1979) *Lake Superior Shipwrecks*. Lake Superior Port Cities Inc., Duluth, Minnesota.